CW00342351

Great Climate

GREAT CLIMATE
Michael Wilding

faber and faber

LONDON · BOSTON

This collection first published in 1990
by Faber and Faber Limited
3 Queen Square London WC1N 3AU

Phototypeset by Parker Typesetting Service, Leicester
Printed in Great Britain by
Clays Ltd, St Ives plc

All rights reserved

© Michael Wilding, 1972, 1975, 1976, 1984

'Joe's Absence' and 'Aspects of the Dying Process'
from *Aspects of the Dying Process*
First published by the University of Queensland Press (1972)

'The West Midland Underground', 'The Man of Slow Feeling',
'Hector and Freddie' and 'See You Later' from *West Midland
Underground*
First published by the University of Queensland Press (1975)

'The Girl Behind the Bar is Reading Jack Kerouac',
'The Vampire's Assistant at the 157 Steps' and 'Her Most
Bizarre Sexual Experience' from *Scenic Drive*
First published by Wild and Woolley (1976)
'Reading the Signs' was published in *The New Yorker*

'Beach Report', 'Reading the Signs' and 'Never Hesitate
to Open Up a File on a Friend' from *Reading the Signs*
First published by Hale and Iremonger (1984)

Michael Wilding is hereby identified as author of this work
in accordance with Section 77 of the Copyright, Designs and
Patents Act 1988

A CIP record for this book is available from the British Library

ISBN 0-571-14428-4

Contents

Beach Report

We woke up in the night when the whole house shook. At first we felt consternation. Not so much terror as consternation. The navy bombarding us with microwaves was one of our first thoughts. Then we decided it was probably psychic emanations from one of the local covens. We put up our own psychic counter-protection, checked that the garlic was still on the window sills, and went back to sleep.

In the morning the landlord told us it was an earth tremor and we felt exhilarated. Then the afternoon papers said QUAKE ROCKS STATE and we felt even better. Now it was the beginning of the end.

When the tidal wave rumours started we all went down to meet it. The wave. The state governor went down with us to assuage the rumours. He took a swim to prove he wasn't concerned.

'Ah, Guv,' we said, 'you have us wrong, we are not concerned, we haven't assembled here in fear. Those in fear have taken to the hills.'

The roads to the hills were scenes of mass carnage as those in fear roared away from the coast and collided with those roaring in joyful anticipation to the beach.

All other things had failed us. Politics, we knew there were no politics, the elections were programmed by the big computers and fed to us on television. Space emigration, we knew there was no space emigration, it was all filmed in California or Arizona or somewhere. As for drugs, now we knew that the CIA had supplied all the acid and sprayed all the marijuana, we knew there was little to be gained from drugs. We tried planting our own but it was soon apparent the seeds had been genetically mutated. That's why there were always so many seeds.

So when the earthquakes came and the tidal waves were promised we felt, well, at least it will shake things up, this is the peak experience we've been waiting for, elimination now. Property values went up along the coast and harbour side. The chance of a ringside experience of obliteration was something the rich weren't going to pass up. A few survival freaks headed for the hills as mentioned before, the weak who will inherit the earth. We didn't want to be hanging out with them. Anyway there was always the chance the hills would be as valleys and the sea beds as mountain tops so there was nothing certain about their calculations.

A few fights broke out on the beach between the love people chanting to avert the catastrophe and the majority of us who were peacefully waiting for it, but we kicked sand in their eyes and threw hot dogs and barbecued steaks and other fleshly substances at them and in the end they retreated. Peace was restored. We introduced dune buggy patrols.

Out beyond the surf was a flotilla of yachts where the rich were drinking gin and snorting coke. They figured to get it a few instants before us, but we'd have the added advantage of being pounded not only by the wave but by the broken bits of their boats and bones.

After a few weeks some people started getting restive. So when the big helicopters landed and scuffed up all the sand so it was like a desert sandstorm, they went across to them in curiosity.

'Why wait?' the helicopter commanders said. 'Why laze on the beach getting skin cancers when you could get instant nadir in Europe. Come into the front line for when we drop the big one. Or two. Skin cancer will have nothing on the total brain frying we can promise.'

So a lot of people enlisted, getting bored on the beach, and they figured they might as well see Europe while it was still there, particularly if it was a chance to see Europe go up in flame and smoke, they'd always had this sense of unease about Europe, the heavy trip Europeans always pulled on us and also the feeling it was such a black place it ought to go up in flame and smoke one day, that was only right. And to be there when it happened, to be participating in the holocaust in the dress circle, it was a once in a lifetime chance too good to pass up.

So that did thin out our numbers. The helicopters lifted them off. A few got instant nadir in the lift off when some of the whirlybirds collided and burst into magnificent flame. It was quite exciting really, like a trailer for the big feature to come.

Then there was this great incandescence in the sea. This was a few months later. Time had pretty well stopped, so it's hard to be specific. But there was this great incandescence and then a ball of light in the sky.

'Wow,' we said.

And these UFOs manifested themselves and descended to earth.

We gave obeisance.

'That's OK, earthlings,' they said, 'thanks for your obeisance but don't get sand in your hair, it'll get into the otherwise sterile environment of the saucer and louse up the anti-gravity devices.'

'Do you mean – ?' we said.

'Yes,' they said. Speaking without mouths, right into our minds.

'We're coming with you – ?' we said, mouthless also, mindless even, we heard ourselves saying it in their minds before we had even thought it.

It was so beautiful. Saucerlings to think for us. Now it was all beyond our control. It was what we had always dreamed, from the first primitive days of television what we had striven for, this surrender to a greater force, the dominance of the subliminal, the freedom from care and struggle.

'Up you get,' they said, raising us all, halt and lame and limping and becrutched and all that, pouring space lotion on our sunburn and skin cancers, combing our hair that turned blond at their touch, fitting us with golden contact lenses for the outreaches of space.

As we stepped into the saucers we had a momentary twinge that we were going to miss the total annihilation by tidal wave.

But it was only momentary. They promised us something even greater. Instant disintegration into particles of electromagnetic energy.

'Wow,' we said, 'the big O, the final solution.'

And they were doing it all for us, for free, we didn't even have to lift a finger.

The Vampire's Assistant
at the 157 Steps

Dexter phones me to get him a woman. Not in the usual sense; not in the sense of get me a woman to screw. A woman to pose for *Vampire Vamp*. Though maybe ultimately it is in the usual sense; he plans to play the part of a young vampire in the book himself. Does that mean he gets to screw the woman?

'I need someone with a certain sort of teeth. Do you know any women vampires?'

My blood has been drained by them. My throat is a necklace of small incisions, like an exotic tattoo from Niugini.

She has to be beautiful and look like a vampire. I thought of Valda but I didn't want her tits and cunt exposed to any more men. There were some books I would prefer to close. Not reissued in runs of 10,000 copies.

'I need a vampire and three guys who get bitten by the vampire. And I need a coffin. Where would I get a coffin from? I only want to borrow one, they can have it back, I'll only need it for three days.'

I suggest he tries an undertaker.

'They won't be in it. They have this thing about the sanctity of death. I guess they're worried about people using them for black masses.'

Dexter needs somewhere to live while he shoots *Vampire Vamp*. He comes to stay with me. Each night he descends the 157 steps down the cliff face, wearing his vampire assistant's make-up, lighting his way with a candle. The dogs in the neighbourhood howl. The possums look down in terror from the gums. At the bottom of the steps, halfway down the cliff, he climbs in through the kitchen window of the fibro house and drags the covers off my bed. There are not enough bedclothes for both of us. Nor is there a duplicate key. When we divide the bedclothes, neither of us is warm enough. He offers to share my bed. I refuse. 'I don't want to fuck you, I just want to sleep in comfort,' he says. I don't trust him. Nor do I want vampire make-up all over the sheets. He refuses to wash it off. Sometimes he says he is too tired. Sometimes he says it saves having to make-up again the next morning. I do not believe either explanation.

Dexter takes the eiderdown and leaves me the blankets. I shiver all night. But it is colder still at Valda's, some sort of swamp having collected under her house owing to bad land drainage which makes the house like a tomb. I pile all her clothes on top of the blankets, coats and sweaters and scarves, but they always fall off in the night and I wake up. The bed slopes to one side. She refuses to believe that. She denies that that is the reason I cannot sleep. She says there are deeper reasons. Sometimes she says there are shallower reasons, reasons that are perfectly visible. But it is never the fault of her bed. As for sleeping at Faith's, that is cold too; she has to keep a window open for her asthma. She also refuses to draw the curtains, so that the light can wake her at seven to get ready for work at nine. Then I have to leave. She does not like leaving me in the apartment alone.

Dexter climbs in through the window and takes the eiderdown about two a.m. He leaves about seven thirty. But at least I don't have to fuck him. I can get back to sleep after he finishes squeezing his fruit juice and making phone calls to his models and his photographer.

'I don't need sleep any more,' Dexter says. 'I sleep for two or three hours but I don't even need that. Alcohol doesn't affect me. I still enjoy it, but I don't get drunk. Dope too. I can smoke dope and then I can carry on working. I stopped eating for three weeks. Just drank water and fruit juice occasionally. You don't need all these things.'

He gets up at three a.m. when his alarm rings. My alarm. He has taken the alarm clock so he wakes up. It isn't that he needs it. It is merely a precaution. He switches it off immediately because he is already awake. He gets up and squeezes some fruit juice and begins to make phone calls. He has to start shooting by the dawn light. I call out to him to bring me the eiderdown back if he is finished with it. He isn't. He has it wrapped round him while he makes the phone calls. He expresses surprise at my being awake. 'It's only three o'clock,' he says.

The timber frame house is at the bottom of 157 steps, surrounded by eucalypts. Another 157 steps further is the water of the bay. The cliff face is nearly vertical. The eucalyptus trees are caught up with the high tension electricity cables, and the branches have frayed the insulation off them. At night I wake up screaming that the wires have been lowered through the roof onto me in bed, that the cliff face has collapsed and the ground is alive with fallen cables. I leap out of bed and switch on the light and look for the cables across the blankets. I get back into bed and realize how dangerous an act that was. Next time I lie there rigid, waiting for the moon to seep through the blinds to reveal where the cables have fallen. With the slightest move I could be fried. Splat.

The lights illuminating the 157 steps suddenly do not work. I descend the vertical cliff face in fear, holding on to twigs and rocks, alert for lizards, snakes, spiders, as I clutch onto things. I stop at every second or third step and look upwards for the cables, but the night is so black I can see nothing. If the lights are not working then the cables must have been rubbed right through by the eucalypts and will now be lying across the steps. I look out to see where they have fallen. I listen for an electric hissing, I watch out for sparks, I wait to die like a flying-fox, spread across two high tension cables.

Dexter tells me the Electricity Board have been. They came to check the safety of the cables. They have checked the wrong cables, the good ones, the ones that light the 157 steps. They have condemned them as unsafe. They have removed some

7

vital link. We must now descend the steps in darkness. We hear the high tension cables still rubbing unchecked against the eucalypts as we walk beneath them.

It is hard to light your way down 157 steps of bush with matches. This is not because they blow out, though sometimes they do blow out. Nor is it because of the danger of bushfire. This could be a danger in bushfire weather. But this is not bushfire weather. The rain drips off every leaf. The moss spreads across every step. The difficulty is not because of bush-fires. The difficulty is knowing where to hold the match so that it illuminates the steps. If you hold the match in front of you it illuminates the steps for beetles and bull ants and lizards lodged in the rocks and tree roots. But your eyes are blinded by the light of the match and you cannot see the steps. If you try the obvious reversal and hold the match behind you, where you have been is illuminated but where you have to go is blocked by your shadow. Your shadow makes it very dark. The steps descend vertically. They are slippery with rain and moss and crushed snails. You grab onto a branch and water showers down from the trees and ticks lodge in your head and neck. You reach out the other side and there is nothing. Eventually you learn to stand a little to one side of the light. There is an optimum angle, height, distance at which to hold the lighted match. You learn to memorize the steps immediately in front of you before the match burns out. That way you save matches. If you can walk four steps into the imprinted, illuminated image after the match goes out, you save a lot of matches.

It is better to descend the 157 steps by candlelight, but Dexter has the only candle. Better still, to descend them by daylight. But then you have to take in supplies because descending by daylight in those short subtropical days you would not have eaten an evening meal, not while it was still daylight. So descending by daylight you end up getting hungry in the long cold evenings. Then you might even have to ascend the steps by matchlight. In order to purchase supplies. It is like living in a state of siege here, without supplies; or in a state of curfew, without light. 'I recognize all this,' Dexter says. 'What a depressing sight it is. When my last woman left me I lived like this for two months.' Without supplies, without curtains, without crockery or cutlery, without all those indefinable things whose absence creates the bareness. I have in fact two curtains left, though the room Dexter sleeps in has bare windows. I have some crockery and cutlery. I have two fridges. One works. The other I guess no one wanted to carry up to the top of the 157 steps when it stopped working. It used to be used to store vegetables. I do not buy vegetables, nor use those remaining. It seems now full of potatoes and onions and other root and tuber crops sprouting in the darkness of its closed doors. Inside it is shining white which is odd when you see the long wavy shoots that have sprouted from the root and tuber crops. But with the door shut it must be very dark. I now feel guilty about those potatoes and onions and things. I feel I should have planted them to let the life they have drawn from themselves spread into the soil and flourish. They are doomed in that old fridge. They are probably dead altogether now, rotted, mouldered. But for a while they drew on their stored life and sprouted in that white-walled darkness.

In winter it is cold here. The sun shines on the other cliff across the bay; this cliff remains damp and shaded all day. Once in the house there is nothing to do but sleep. There is no television; it is too steep to carry a set down. It is too cold to read.

I come home early to sleep. It has become impossible to sleep at night without blankets, and with Dexter making phone calls. I find Dexter lying on the floor, across the doorways to his room and to my room. The doorways are close to each other. He has the electric radiator on, the one bar of it that works. The lights are off. His head rests on a pillow, and he is covered by the eiderdown. His shoulders sticking out above the eiderdown are clad in his duffle coat. He doesn't answer when I say hello. I step over him and switch on a light. I step back. He still does not move. I am shocked by the way he has aged, I feel a deep physical shock at the lines round his eyes, the dark hollows

9

beneath them, the black dead flesh. He looks centuries old.

'Why are you lying there like that?' I ask. 'Why don't you go to bed if you're so tired?'

'I'm all right like this,' he says.

'It can't be comfortable.'

'I'm going to make a phone call.'

'Why don't you make it then and go to bed?'

'Not yet.'

'The phone won't move, you don't have to lie on guard by it.'

He wriggles into his eiderdown but does not open his eyes.

I lie in bed. The glow of the electric radiator comes through the doorway. I have come home early to sleep and I cannot sleep. I tell myself that it is not age on Dexter's face. We are not that near to death. It is the work of a brilliantly gifted make-up artist. It is very hard to sleep when someone who could be a vampire is lying across the doorway to your room. Even a trainee vampire. When the doorway has no door. When you don't have an eiderdown to wrap protectively round your throat. Apart from the additional fear of fire, that he might roll onto the electric radiator and ignite the eiderdown and himself and yourself; myself. Like Nosferatu in the first rays of dawn. What if he forgot his phone call and lay there all night in his duffle coat and eiderdown and eye make-up and the rosy fingers stretched across Middle Harbour and gently touched him? Pow.

This suburb that looks over the harbour must once have been a place for weekenders. Now the city has caught up with it and absorbed it and gone on way past it. But once it was a place to put little shacks and to come away to for the fishing. The house is of prefabricated fibro. The materials decay yet never blend. A timber house yearns back to the growing trees around it. But the hard edges of this fibro stay for ever hard, the metal window frames rust but never soften; they flake, they chip away, they support cobwebs. Lianas hang from the trees, lizards and insects scurry, possums leap on the corrugated iron roof. The house stays there, this cold, hard unbending cube. It asserts the origins of its manufacture in this flux of the bush. It is functional, minimal, technological. It provided quick and cheap happiness where there might not have been happiness: but when the happiness faded it could not sustain it. It is prefabricated and temporary: it will collapse but not decay. Like a Mayan temple overgrown in the jungle, it is a monument to a creed; it is a statue to loss of faith. The sun sets across the bay and its last rays reach the windows; the moon rises and lights them too. We sit there listening to the radio and smoking dope. We sit close to the window and do not see the house around us, back of us. We sit in folding deck chairs because no other chairs have been carried down the steps.

Some nights when the moon is late rising Dexter shows me his transparencies. He shows me *Chained* in which a beautiful woman is immured in a deserted castle. She is naked and chained by her wrists to the wall of the dungeon. Each day her captor comes to whip her. He is the only person she sees. In her loneliness she looks forward to his brief visits. The whipping becomes the joy of her life.

The fridge that works is overfreezing. The cartons of milk go solid overnight. To make tea you have to scoop out solid milk. It strikes me as a possible new way of packaging: quick frozen milk cubes. They could be condensed and flavoured. Chocolate, coffee, malt, vanilla, lemon, herbal.

My pyjamas have a thick congealed substance on them. It is not frozen milk, otherwise it would have melted. I wonder what discharge this is. I usually examine my prick for discharges. I wonder if some come in the night. I wonder if when I masturbate strange new pusses emerge that I am unaware of. I carry this fear with me through the days that follow. I later decide I must have sat on the kitchen table where Dexter has spilt hot candle wax, climbing through the window. I take my pyjamas to the laundry and the symptoms never recur.

As I climb up the 157 steps and come in sight of the road, I see an old chair on the pathway. The steps wind up the vertical cliff and I see angle after angle of the wooden chair. Its odd construction reveals it to be a commode. I do not want an old chair full of shit blocking the way out of the house. I do not want to touch it. Old, forgotten diseases might lurk in it. I wonder why it has been dumped on my steps. I did not think my neighbours had the imagination. They have not previously gone beyond sitting at their window with a rifle and threatening to shoot guests at my party.

It could accidently have been dumped there. Yet why on my steps? Why not just sit on the side of the road? I do not like to think of all those sick and aged people who have shitted into it. Though it does not seem to have been used recently. The wood appears to be distinctly weathered. It seems to have been exposed to the sun and rain for some time. I carry it across the road and wipe my hands on the grass.

When I come home at night it is back on the steps. I pick it up with one hand and carry it across the road from my steps again and dump it in the bush there. All evening I feel this anxiety. I cannot interpret the old commode on the steps. I cannot find its signification. I go round the house and secure all the doors and windows; except for the kitchen window which I have to leave open for Dexter. I do not like leaving the kitchen window open but there is nothing else I can do.

In the morning the chair is back on the steps.

In the evening Dexter says: 'You know there's something funny going on round here. That old commode, someone keeps moving it around.'

'Yes,' I say. I hadn't wanted to talk about it. I had hoped it was an hallucination. I would prefer to be mentally sick than have someone persecute me with an old commode.

'I found it on this tip when we were shooting *Garbo Girl* and I thought what a tremendous prop. But I didn't want to bring it right down the stairs and have to carry it back up when I go.'

At least he still has the concept of going.

The next morning there is a circular in the letter box. 'Dear Neighbour, One of our neighbour's daughters has been raped in this street. We are calling a meeting to arrange for more police protection in this area. We invite you to attend.'

I do not ask Dexter if he can explain that mystery too. I keep the letter from him. I wish he would go soon. I am afraid the neighbours will burn the house down if they work out he is living here. We are such natural suspects, such natural victims.

The next morning I find that someone has shitted at the top of the steps, and the commode has gone altogether.

Never Hesitate to Open up
a File on a Friend

'I tell you my maxim. It's some French fellow's too, I believe, but that don't matter – divide to conquer. Set all the dogs spying on each other . . . if the prisoners were as faithful to each other as we are, we couldn't hold the island a week. It's just because no man can trust his neighbour that every mutiny falls to the ground.'

Marcus Clarke, *His Natural Life*

The problem is that though you realize it would be a good idea not to use so much dope, and not only financially, but in the area of the lungs, just smoking, the aches across the chest, the deep irritation in the back, and when you do manage not to have a smoke till five p.m. you feel so good, at five p.m. you get such a blast, instead of being so stoned by then that it needs two or three joints to get over just driving through the traffic, but the problem is, though you realize all this, and resolve, it is the ache that gets you, the ache along your teeth, through your bones, your joints, across your skull, not withdrawal but the ache of living, perceived, and you need something to numb that ache, and this way all the resolutions go. All you can do is spend a moment in silent gratitude that it isn't smack. And anyway people who knew you elsewhere remember your aspirin habit and your codeine habit and you yourself remember the alcohol habit and that doesn't do your stomach any good let alone the rest of you, so despite all these resolutions there is this ache, this ache of living perceived.

So you sit around waiting until you know your friendly neighbourhood dealer will be home, he doing a job in the nine to five hours, the dealing being more moonlighting now than anything else, a way to get a bit of cash together and put a deposit on a place to live, that's where you went wrong, getting into the property thing, friendly neighbourhood dealer, friendly for short, frend even, not that at the time we didn't call him by his name, but now we're not so eager to use names, not in this context. And there's no point going round to see him till the traffic's cleared, so you drop in to visit someone else closer who might have a smoke, he does have a smoke, and then the glow reappears, that vibrancy in the air, the life in the timber's grain. 'Why don't you put some on one side,' says this person I visit, 'buy a block and put some away for a rainy day.' 'It's always a rainy day somewhere,' I point out. I weep for the unacknowledged rainy days around the world.

In fact this presumably being one of those days without a smoke till five p.m. that I feel so good at this post five p.m. point that I even go down to the pub and never get across to Frend's. I stay there and get drunk, the band plays 'You make me feel so good', the singer brings tears to my eyes, 'You make me feel so good', she sucks us into these great walls of sadness, the aura of smack circles around them like a black halo, the bass player has an evil eye tonight, the guitarist turns his back on us and plays to the wall, and the singer sings 'You make me feel so good' and brings tears to our eyes. It's hard writing without using names, but that's how it is if you're going to say the band's on the nod. And so another nameless person is sitting at the bar and wraps an arm round you and you round her, she is being ample at the bar, Arabella's amplitudes, do you have supplies, yessir we have ample, do you have anything to cook it on, no sir we'll have raw ample, I used to cycle home midday from school and the goon show would be on while I ate my apple crumble and in the evening I'd read Thomas Hardy, come back for a drink, she says, before she leaves, which I do, but drop up the road for a smoke first and pick up a deal from another friend I meet in the pub, so that I don't need to get over to Frend's. This is the first time in a year I've gone down to the pub and got drunk and fucked someone like we used to do all the time back in the drinking days.

So at or around the point I don't drive over to Frend's he is sitting watching TV with his hookah and his dope stash there on the table and the seagrass matting floor covered with books and newspapers and a couple of prints on the otherwise bare walls, he liked that bare, bachelor, anchoritic effect, and the door's kicked in by eight dees and the person he's doing a big deal with at that precise moment runs out of the door, through this bunch of eight dees coming along the narrow hallway, and escapes, while the eight dees pistol whip Frend around the face, taking something out of the telephone receiver, and gather together his dope and his wine. The wine he felt particularly incensed about. So they only charge you with a third or half the amount of dope there was, that's good, it lessens the heinousness of the crime so though it pisses you off that they're ripping it off to resell, at least it gives you a better chance, and they'll no doubt resell the declared amount later too. But the wine, knocking off the wine made him very sore.

I get drunk, get a fuck, score some dope and don't get busted, why should I be so lucky? And save petrol too.

I drop in to see Frend at his place of work which like so much else is best remaining anonymous, lovingly rendered realism is not for the age of paranoia, and we walk up the street looking for a place to sit and talk and have coffee, these are the places that no longer exist, so we find a hamburger joint and drink our coffee there, having tramped a quarter of a mile up the street and back again. 'How did you know?' he said, 'Nemo told me,' 'Fucker,' he says, 'no reflection on you,' he says, 'but he wasn't supposed to tell anyone, it's not that I've got anything against you personally,' he says, 'but you know how it is, just the fewer people who know, and with the people you know, you know, and the job.' 'I know,' I said, 'that's fine, I understand.' Paranoia is no stranger to me. 'Fucker,' he said, 'anyway, you won't say anything.'

He looks terrible, Frend, there are deep black scimitars beneath his eyes, standing pools of blackness, and his eyes focus on the sugar, the coffee, the table. Someone comes in to the hamburger joint I recognize, sitting at the table behind us, so we talk about other things, what other things are there to talk about, sitting there, our eyes scanning the street, looking over shoulders.

'I might need to borrow some bail money at some time, if things go bad,' he says. 'Sure,' I say. Generally this gets paid back. I'm still owed seventeen dollars bail money for someone or other, one of those Saturday night whip rounds when all I had was seventeen dollars, which is a good policy, not to have more than seventeen dollars in cash. The people who get busted on Saturday night drunk driving tend to be not too good a risk. And I've refused the last couple of times to lend thirty dollars for a hit to a desperate junkie and it's on my conscience but you can start lending those thirty dollars and it stops coming back. So 'Sure' I say to Frend, 'sure'. 'It might be a few hundred, but I've worked it out, I've worked out a system for paying back.' 'Sure,' I say. 'And I might need a character reference,' he says. I have known Mr Frend for some seven years and have always found him a reliable, honest, conscientious, hard-working citizen . . .

And all we want to do is sit looking over the harbour, the prawn trawlers chugging past in the evenings, the yachts at weekends, the barges piled with timber, the floating cranes, the naval ships firing off blanks, we hope they're blanks, the Maritime Services Board boats, the police boats, all we want to do is watch this activity, not even engage with it, sit here gently smoking as the day revolves. Sometimes there are oil spillages and the fire boats come by and spray detergent on the waters. Sometimes there are rainbows, rainbows arcing over the arc of the harbour bridge, and beneath it, right through and beyond and out at the ocean the lighthouse winks through the night. And little spirals of smoke rise from our seats in the window here, as we sink lower out of sight, just these gentle spirals of the peace pipe.

And for this they come and kick in doors. 'It's these fucking feds,' says Frend, 'they do psychology courses and watch American police series on TV, they're fucking beasts.' It used to be such a value-free word but it got so associated with the apocalypse, beast of, they had to dig up animal to replace it so they had a word with none of those 666 connotations. 'So how did they get you?' you ask and he says, 'I've been thinking about that.' 'Figured you might,' you say. 'I think it was this friend of Nemo's.' 'Nemo's?' you say. 'He should've been more careful, I'm pissed off with him at not, you know, it's not warning, you can't warn everyone about everyone, but you can remind them, if you think it's slipped their memory you ought to remind them, nothing heavy, but he should have reminded me about this guy.' There is a store of common information and we should keep turning it over, grubbing through it like pigs in shit. 'Don't talk about pigs,' says Frend. But pigs are what we should've talked about a lot more. 'It's these fucking police agents,' he says, 'that's the system they've got, so one pig runs maybe ten agents, apart from the people they bust and turn, well a lot of the agents they got by busting them, then they offer them a deal. They offered me a deal,' he says, 'but as soon as they saw I wasn't buying it they dropped it.' 'What sort of deal?' 'Oh, you know, where did it come from.' 'So what did you say?' 'I said I didn't know, somebody I met in a bar.' 'They believe you?' 'Not really, no,' he says, 'but I stuck to it, it was the best I could come up with.' All the stories we tell and we don't have any good ones stacked in reserve. 'So it was a friend of Nemo's?' 'Well, not a friend exactly, someone he knew, and he knew how weak he was, he'd been busted, they'd threatened to take his kids away, the usual stuff, Nemo told me this later, why didn't he tell me before?' 'And he was the guy who got away?' 'No, he wasn't there, he put me on to the guy who ran away.' 'Who was a cop.' 'Yeah,' says Frend, 'it looks like it.' 'And where does Nemo fit in?' 'He was getting the stuff in the first place.' You can see why the stuff's so fucking expensive with everyone taking a cut and no one wanting to actually be doing the deal, actually touch the stuff with their bare fingerprints, except the poor growers who get ripped off or hung up by their toes and then ripped off, but this is just capitalism, one of the last areas of primary accumulation being taken over by the monopoly phase.

These are the days we aren't in much. Or when we are in, not answering the door much. Rearranging the curtains so the window where they used to look in when they knocked the door or rang the bell is curtained over now. And tiny rips in it to look out by but not in through. This we have in common for our various reasons, Frend and me, being less at home. The door no longer open letting the winds clear the room; but the still air, the clouds of doubt above the chinese paper lanterns, curling round the picture rail, hanging down from the ceiling's corners. This we share, Frend and me, the corrosive doubt. Whoever it was, a friend set him up. Falling into bad company, he calls it. The bad companions of these otherwise gentle days. But there's still enough dope to keep an edge of gentleness, soften out the jangling, which maybe we softened out too much.

We run through the stories again, the amazing escape through the eight dees coming along the hallway, the pistol whipping, the knocked-off wine, and the other person who Nemo should have warned about, busted at the same time for a couple of ounces of hash and a few plants in the back yard. 'To make it look good,' says Frend, 'they had to make it look good.' And the phone still has the clicks even though the house has fewer visitors, many fewer visitors. And we talk about the friends we doubt, never announcing we doubt them, but just for them to be talked about, the mark of our doubt.

These are the days when people don't come round, when the people you suspect you suspect know you suspect them so don't come round, they could just think you're suddenly hostile, but they don't come round, so you sit in the window watching the sailing boats capsize in the weekend winds, and you take down the crystal ball from where it hangs through the lampshade, designed to refract the light into prismatic splinters when you're tripping, but in this state of paranoia you prefer not to trip, so you use it as a pendulum. Are Arthur, Bill, Charlie, Denis, Evelyn, Fred, George, Harry, Ian, Jose, Kevin, Larry, Michael, Norm, Olaf, Pierre, Qwerty, Rolf, Sam, Trudi, Uri, Vern, Walter, Xiannis, Yoni and Zoe police agents, circling clockwise, positive, anti-clockwise, negative, but it becomes absurd, the clockwise spinning, too extreme to record and where would you record it and hide it. So you do it. Should I visit Marg, Stu, Frend, Blue, and once again you stay in, a

Friday night and you stay in, a Saturday night and you stay in, a Sunday afternoon and you watch the sailing boats capsize on the harbour. Sometimes you deny it, sometimes you figure you can't ask the pendulum shoulds, only is's, so you drive round to Frend's anyway and he's not in, so maybe the message merely meant you shouldn't visit because it would be a waste of time, he wouldn't be there. And his eyes darken, the crescents deepen beneath them, his nose narrows into a scimitar as he chain smokes. 'Your aura's not very good,' says Lily, 'are you smoking a lot?' We have this feeling of the net again, the intrusion, the penetration, particularly when the phone goes off for five days and the day it comes back on Lily's goes off for twelve. These things make you ask where you can ask. Once you've felt the vampire at your neck, you recognize the feeling. One reason you don't like fucking strangers is the way they kiss at the jugular.

He phones up and says he'll drop round and you say you'll be in. You are in. You don't know what to do but maybe you'll check it out, check the eyes, disinformation has to convey information as its base, disinformation can be decoded. But when he comes up the step you hear him talking to someone and you don't answer the door, you hear the knock, of course you hear the fucking knock, but you stand still in the room, breathing quietly, waiting till they go, they go.

'You not answering the door these days?' he says, when you answer the phone and it's Frend. 'Oh, you know,' you say, 'yes and no, sometimes.' 'I came round the other night.' 'Yeah,' you say. 'I figured you were there but not answering, fair enough.' 'Just working on my intuitions,' you say. And there are a couple of sentences more which you can't remember now, which is a pity since they were the last sentences you heard him say, nothing dramatic, he still says sentences to other people, but to you, that was the last dialogue and you don't remember it and he doesn't phone or come round again.

20

Joe's Absence

Driving through the bush, past the level sweeps of still gums, motionless, silent on the bright windless day, Graham began to wonder why he didn't live permanently out here somewhere, away from drinking too much and writing too little and going to movies the only nights he didn't go to the pub or a party. Joe had stood in the pub five o'clock on Friday, his skin browned, his hair bleached light at the tips from the sun, announcing, as they were crushed into the corner between the cigarette machine and the wall, that he had written a dozen stories in the last two months. Graham was about to ask how many of these were rewrites, not having written a dozen in two years unless you counted the abortive novel as several, but Helen had started to giggle and nudge Pat seeing him and Joe wedged in and talking. She'd never really forgiven Joe for dropping her, or him for knocking her back after a party one night. So Joe pushed through the crowd to put his arms round Helen and Pat, and Graham moved along to where he could see some other girl's head, and pinch her bottom affectionately.

When the pub had thinned out a bit about a quarter to eight, he could see Joe again, in his jeans and ex-army bush shirt, shouted drinks by all the people he hadn't seen for so long, coming up so rarely now, leaning against the bar with the peace of a beachcomber.

'So why don't you come down?' he said. 'You can stay there, there's two rooms.'

'I might. So how many have you sold?'

'I'm not; I'm putting them into a collection. I'm not trying the magazines. I'm keeping them till I've got them all ready to publish at once.'

'You write all day?'

'In the mornings; then in the afternoons I usually go to the beach and swim and read and lie in the sun; sometimes I write in the evening; it depends; sometimes I just make notes. Then there's Margot.'

'Then there's Margot.'

'She keeps me company.'

The gums were high and never seemed to have any birds in them, no movement, no rustling; yet they must have done; perhaps if he stopped the car and got out and watched, he would notice some. But just looking as he drove past, he could see nothing moving at all, just that huge stretching silence, reaching over soil and rocks no one had ever stepped on. It was frightening when you thought of all that emptiness reaching right out into the centre, it was frightening like looking at the stars was frightening, the terror of those inconceivable distances. It was the terror that made you cluster in the cities, clinging like ants on a dead lizard's sore, sucking sustenance from the skin's small crack.

Yet Joe had been able to give it away. He rarely came to the pub now. But stabbed reams of white paper with neat black characters, sheet after sheet, and in the afternoons lay on the beach, casually trickling through his fingers the innumerable grains of sand, sleeping at night between the immense silence of the sea, and the mute stillness of the bush.

With Margot, of course.

Margot had come into the pub later and he'd hardly noticed her. She'd nestled round Joe and started to talk to him quietly.

'Meet Graham,' Joe had said, and she smiled and said Hello Graham and carried on talking.

'Graham's coming down to stay with us,' Joe had said.

She smiled again; good teeth; and carried on talking to Joe. She spoke too quietly for Graham to hear anything; Joe seemed to resent her doing that, being secretive, so spoke loudly.

'All right,' he said, with the same volume he had used to introduce Graham. 'I'm not stopping you; go on; go and have dinner with your friend.'

She smiled at him and went out, waving.

'We have a free relationship,' Joe said. 'She's gone off to screw some old friend.' He ordered two more middies, and later intercepted Helen and Pat as they were leaving so that they all went for a meal together, and after the pub closed went on to a party.

A few houses clustered round the edge of the bay, with a shop that did duty as a post office. He drove past, following Joe's directions of turning up a track past the houses. Where the track stopped was the house.

He left the car on the rough road, and walked to a gap in amongst clusters of lantana where a piece of broken board nailed to a post indicated the house. Joe's burnt poker work had marked it 75, as an urban affirmation. But the house was rough stone thrown together, like a cairn marking a food cache, or a body unburiable because of the rocky ground. It had a window and a door, and a corrugated iron shed roof on top of the blocks of stone. It was about big enough to hold a small car. All around was scrub.

The door was shut, locked. Graham looked through the window on to a bench with a typewriter, a sheet of paper in the carriage. He could not read what had been written because the typist had been facing the window.

He walked round the shack, seeing only bush stretching in every direction, blue, grey, green, dusty, mile upon mile. A kookaburra called out, just once, and everything was quiet after its mechanical harshness.

Stopped back at the beach he leant his elbows on the top of the open car door, and looked for Joe. He liked the look of the beach; all that sand, all that water; for an afternoon at least it would be pleasant, talking to Joe. Watching the occasional girl, perhaps. There was one in a yellow bikini, lying on her stomach, her legs spread apart, a book propped in front of her on a heap of scooped sand, her chin resting on her fists, one hand above the other. She might have been asleep or looking at the sea. He swept his eyes from her, like a withdrawing wave, and examined the few groups of people lying in the sun; a middle-aged mother with three children, two old men walking, a group of five or six teenagers.

'It's like Big Sur,' Joe had said at the party.

His eyes drew over the girl again, an impersonal wave, but ready to settle. She must have felt him; she swivelled round on her belly, looked over her shoulder, her eyes engaging with his. Seeing her face he wondered if it was Margot. Even if not, to ask her would inaugurate a conversation. Having driven so far, the least he could do was have a conversation.

'I thought I'd seen you somewhere,' she said. Her voice was young, welcoming, unguarded. But as it was Margot he stopped evaluating the curve of her hips, the flow of her legs, and sat down on the sand.

'Have a towel,' she said. 'I've got two.'

He sat on it, though the sand was dry.

'What are you doing?' she asked.

'I came down to see you.'

'Me?' She cocked her head on one side and smiled at him, as if she were pleased.

'Well, Joe and you, yes.'

'Oh, pity,' she said. 'I think he's in town.'

'Christ, he told me he'd be here; he bloody well invited me down.'

She shrugged her shoulders and turned the book face down. 'He stayed in town last night. He had to see someone or something today. I thought he might have been seeing you.'

'So did I.'

She pulled a face. 'He might come back on the ferry for lunch if he said he'd see you here,' she said.

'When's that?'

'I don't know; I never carry a watch. I sort of like to forget time down here.' She stretched her arms out, yawning from the comfortable sun, wriggling her wrists as she gave a final reaching stretch, and then lay on her stomach again. 'Why don't you sunbathe?' she said.

She began reading her book. Graham took off his shirt and used it to lay his head on, and kicked off his thongs. He had no shorts with him, so lay in his jeans, too tight to roll up. He watched her, but dragged his mind away to Joe's last bird. He'd gone for Lydia. She'd been much more attractive than this one. It might be worth doing something about it now; he'd ask Joe her address. He'd only made a line for her once; that didn't count the first time he saw her at that conference he'd talked at. They'd all had several beers over lunch, and he'd stayed on for the afternoon paper, sitting next to Lydia, because Joe wanted to be in the front to attack the speaker. They'd grinned at each other every time either of them nearly fell asleep. It was the time after, when he and Joe had talked at some literary festival about new directions in literature, that he'd made the line. Funny how no one else had noticed it sounded like nude erections. They'd been given a bottle of grog each in lieu of payment; Joe got whisky and he got brandy, by moving quickly and not looking at the wine labels; at the party afterwards after the pub had shut he shared his brandy with Lydia, telling her she should relax more, be less frigid, more swinging. She kissed him to convince him she was. But either he or she or Joe had got wound up with somebody else and that was the end of the evening. And he'd not seen her since. This new one, Margot, didn't seem as frigid, as aloof. He couldn't decide how less attractive she was. Her breasts were fuller than he'd remembered. He liked full breasts and small bottoms. She had small feet that she curled, turning the toes over so that the soles of the feet moved, the skin wrinkling, tensing, relaxing, as if it were being gently tickled.

'It's a beaut place,' she said. She had put her book down and was looking at Graham who lay watching her, wondering after all. 'It's quiet and there's hardly anyone here except in the school holidays. Then they come down a bit. But not much. And you don't get the surfies; the bay breaks the waves, so they can't surf here. That land along there sweeps round as a sort of arm of the bay.' She half raised herself to point towards the sea, her breasts lifted so that their tips just touched the sand. 'Sometimes there isn't anyone here at all, just Joe and me. And around the corner' – and she sat up, resting on her left arm and with her back towards him, pointed out beyond where their view was blocked by the close, wooded rise at the bay's edge – 'there's another bay that you hardly see anyone on at all. It's almost totally deserted' – and the tanned skin of her shoulders rippled. Having pointed she stretched herself again, the line of her back arching, her hair dropping back, hanging over but not touching her shoulders, as she bent her head right back. She rubbed her eyes, watery from yawning, and then lay down, sunning her stomach. She tipped her head on one side to look at him while she talked. 'I've been so sort of healthy since I've been here, swimming and lying on the beach and walking, walking miles, along the beaches, stretching on and on, miles of gleaming sand. If you walk below the tideline you can see your foot tracks just one line, stretching right out of sight. It's quite eerie in a way. Just you and the sea and the sand.' Her breasts rose when she breathed in deeply, breathing in fully and smiling, content. Her stomach was flat, downy, the downy hair glistening golden in the sun. Grains of sand clung to it in little patches. She scuffed hollows for her heels to settle in. 'You'd think Joe would be the sort of person who'd hate it, but he's crazy about it. He's written a dozen stories, and he's got a stack of notes for others he keeps leafing through. They're much better than anything he did before. At least, I think they are. I didn't know him before, but I've looked at some of the things he wrote then. And they're not as good. Not as good as these he's writing now.' She raised her bottom off the sand, her weight on her shoulders and feet, for no other reason than that in the sun she felt healthy, active. 'That's the ferry,' she said, rolling on to her stomach again, leaning her breasts on her folded arms and watching the small boat approach the landing jetty at the right of the bay, beneath the slight, sloping promontory. 'Joe'll probably be on this if he's coming back for lunch.'

He stopped looking at her and watched the arriving ferry, being impersonal, and asked, 'What are Joe's stories about? The same themes?' Restraining a pejorative old.

'Joe, of course,' she smiled at him.

One of the crew threw a rope from the ferry round the wharf post.

'What do you do?' she asked, conversationally.

He turned back from the sea to her. He wondered why Joe hadn't told her; or whether she'd not bothered to remember. He said, slowly, 'I write; a bit; not so prolifically as Joe seems to be doing.'

'He never has before, he says,' she said, as if to touch his arm consolingly.

He watched the gangplank being thrust from the gap between the rail across on to the jetty.

'No,' he said.

'What sort of things do you write?' she asked, probably as she'd first asked Joe. It was a good opening and he'd followed surely along it before. But he just looked at the passengers crossing the gangplank and the minibus backing to meet them. 'Stories,' he said, watching for Joe to arrive.

She borrowed five cents for the phone, and he watched her walk to the road, the line of her bikini on her hips rising and dipping to alternate sides with each step, a yellow sun receding, alone distinguishable as the bra strap was only a narrow cord. Instead of returning directly, she walked diagonally across from the road to the water and swam, as if he had not been there at all. And when she swam underwater nothing remained to show she ever had been there, except her towel and book beside him. He wondered idly what the book was, but did not bother to reach for it. He lay prostrate, facing the sea, watching her head occasionally surface, and then her head and neck emerge, her breasts, her hips, her thighs, and soon she was running up the beach, bending over him to pick up her towel, water dripping from her hair on to his hot back, running in rivulets down her neck and throat, over her breasts in separate runnels that met between them, in trickles over her belly and thighs. She shook her head, her hair flung round scattering drops of water like a dog, drops dampening the white sand to brief disks of mud. He noticed how the elastic of her bikini ran taut across her hips but left two small gaps between the inside of her hips and the rise of her belly. He watched a trickle of water run towards and then away from the gap, and when she bent over to comb her hair it fell from her side to the sand and was lost among the hot grains.

'Joe's in town,' she said, as she lay down again, flat on her stomach, ignoring the towel and lying in the hot sand. She lay down so that they faced each other and their bodies were in a straight line.

'Uh-huh.'

'He's not coming down till tomorrow.'

They looked at each other. He smiled, ruefully for many reasons. She looked straight back at him.

'He must have got so pissed he didn't bother to remember, the bastard,' he said. And even momentarily convinced himself he felt annoyance.

'It's a beaut day, anyway,' she said; and, his chin resting on the sand, her breasts were directly ahead of him. 'At least it won't be wasted.'

'I could have been writing another short story,' he said; 'like Joe.'

'Joe didn't seem to have had time to think of one.'

He wriggled deeper into the sand. How much, after all, had he wanted to talk to Joe, and be competitive about acceptances and women? He thought it would be pleasanter alone with her.

Yet he found her strangely distant; though not consistently. She had swum as if he had not been there, but after they had eaten crisps and cashew nuts and chocolate which they bought at the shop, she suggested they should go to the other beach which was always deserted.

They walked between lines of shells, stopping to examine those with fine colours or rare shapes, or to touch twigs rounded and smoothed by the tides. No houses reached on to the beach, no roads passed it. The waves broke gently on the sand, the only sound. The bush stood still at the beach's edge.

It was not a physical distance. They walked along together leaving an irregular, merging, quadruped track, sometimes bumping against each other when one of them stopped or crossed in front of the other for a shell or fragment of coral; and she would halt him by touching his lower arm when in front of them a single claw probed through a sand hole into the air, probed slowly and at their slightest movement dropped out of sight. But there was another distance, a sort of obliqueness that disturbed him. Alone on this stretch of beach he felt naked with her, unwatched, unhampered, unprotected by the smallest of societies. The emptiness menaced him, left him without covering or support, and without people to crush against him their solitary closeness on the empty beach seemed like an immense distance. Yet it should have been a closeness. Though asteroids collide despite the infinite spaces, brushing together on that huge strand could not be casual. On the beach when footsteps scuffed into each other's, there must have been some contrivance; which must have implied more than a physical closeness.

But in the emptiness her laughter bounced off the bright sand as if it could never, would never, penetrate. Her laughing, her flinging her hair, her brushing her arm with her breast, her skipping, all the incidents fondling him, stroking his cheeks, relaxing his set eyes, might just have been handstands and cartwheels on firm surfaces.

And Joe?

And Joe, after the coolness and poise of Lydia, might have gone for girlishness; which was distant too, like Lydia.

If it was sexy too.

Space's infinity turns back on itself. Revolves through its first, its perpetual, question. How could he tell if she was sexy?

He laughed to himself; how could he tell if she was sexy! He looked at her, whose inventory he could recite from memory after looking for so long, at her catalogue of movements.

'What are you looking at?' she asked.

'You.'

'When Joe looks like that I know there's going to be trouble.'

'Like he's going to rape you?'

'Not me,' she said. 'That wouldn't be a trouble.'

'Oh, he's all right,' he said; but not restraining a taint of scarcely concealed doubt from lapsing over his voice.

'He's sexy, too,' she said. And then she said, 'I'll race you to that fallen gum.'

Before he could refuse, she had begun running, so he padded after her, the gap between them widening at every gasp.

Joe had said it was just like Big Sur.

He dropped the towel from his neck and her book and comb from his pocket and then flopped down, sweating.

'You should stay here,' she said, 'get healthy.'

He grunted, making slow flailing motions in the sand like a turtle, struggling to pull off his shirt.

'I'm going to have a swim. Why don't you come in?' she said.

He brushed the hair from his forehead for coolness.

'You don't need any trunks here,' she said.

'Sure?' he said, not hastening, not rushing, not sure of her still.

'Sure,' she said. 'I'm going to take off my bikini anyway; it's more sort of, I don't know; I like the feel of the water against me.'

And the waves lapped round them both, fondling them in a joint embrace, while they swam or floated, and when she floated on her back her breasts just rose above the surface, her nipples pink in the silvered blue water.

It was when he lay on the towel, drying in the sun and the wind that was blowing up, that his penis grew stiff and tumescent, joining the heat of his sunburn with a spreading heat of his own. He watched her lying there, her breasts firm, her nipples taut, her stomach flowing in gentle curves to the triangle of her pubic hair, to her open legs. She turned her head on one side and looked at him, and when they both smiled, he reached over a hand and grabbed hers. They competed in the pressure of their grips.

The wind that had blown up brought spots of rain.

'We could do a Lady Chatterley in the storm,' she said, 'or go back to the shack.'

'The shack might be better,' he said. 'Besides, I haven't got any flowers handy.'

Besides, he felt the need to think. And walking along the beach, returning parallel with their double line of footprints, and walking up the bush track that was a short cut, he tried to think, as he bumped against her, or put his arm round her when she seemed likely to make a slightest stumble, the tips of his fingers pressing on her warm body.

How could he be sure Joe wouldn't be back, anyway, or come back on a later ferry, or in a drunken car? But that wasn't it, not the detection. It was screwing her in the first place. Why did Joe always get such attractive birds? He pondered his loyalties to Joe, which needed only to be few. He had Joe's comment that it was a free relationship; and Joe's absence as support. Why wait till Joe dumped her? Why not move in now? What difference was there, except in wasting time?

Though it was Joe, after all; who hadn't two-timed him ever; as far as he knew; and whom he'd never two-timed yet; except perhaps by speaking for twenty minutes at that conference when he'd agreed on ten minutes, and Joe had only ten minutes prepared. And rubbishing his stories privately; but Joe probably reciprocated that.

He watched her hips move, following behind her on the last narrow stretch of the track. A kookaburra called out, and another picked up its cry. They flew off into the bush, still cackling. The rain began to fall heavily so they ran the last stretch to the car.

They stood close to each other as she took the key from under a stone and opened the door. Inside, they held against each other, pressing their bodies into each other. He put his hand against her back, slipping it down to run over her buttocks beneath her bikini. He kissed her and would have steered her to the bed, hoping by haste to forestall thought. But she took one arm away from him and pressed its index finger just beneath his shoulder bone.

'What,' she said, gently pressing for emphasis with each word, 'what about Joe?'

'Since you mention it,' he said, 'I'd been wondering.'

'It's not me as much as you; I know he's going to dump me sometime like he always does; but you're both good friends.'

'We're just good friends,' he said, licking the salt around her ear.

'But seriously,' she said, like a little girl, 'I don't specially want to betray him; but I think he'd be more hurt if you did.'

'Betraying's a bit melodramatic, isn't it?'

'And sexy too.'

He let her go, fondling her stomach when she turned round.

'Why don't we eat first?' she said.

'Could do,' he said, casually, adding, 'I'll be surer then.'

'Surer which way?'

'One way.'

'You're not sure now, are you, at all?'

He replied 'No', but it hadn't been a question; nor something he had wanted to remember.

'I know, I could tell. That's why,' she began; and then gave him a kiss full on the mouth, as if to show she didn't hold it against him; and to stop him from answering.

'I'll make an orgiastic meal,' she said.

'Why, aren't you sure?'

She looked at him: 'I'm always sure,' she said, 'but I'm also hungry.' And she might have been.

She put on her jeans and a sweater and lent him a sweater of Joe's as, now it was raining, it was cold inside. She lit an oil lamp. The walls were bare stone, the floor concrete on which they had thrown rush mats. A hardboard partition served to create two rooms, a bedroom one side, a combined kitchen, eating room, and spare bedroom the other. She cooked on stored gas in one corner. An old mattress lay on the floor for seating and visitors. She brought a flagon of red wine and a couple of glasses from the bedroom, and sat down on the mattress beside him, snuggling against him.

'What's that masterpiece?' he asked, pointing to the typewriter with its sheet of quarto.

'Why don't you have a look?' she said; but it was warm against her and she might relent, before eating.

He drank some of the wine and shrugged his shoulders. And added, 'I don't like anyone looking at what I'm working on. I don't even like them reading it in typescript when it's finished. It's a sort of intrusion. It makes me feel exposed and vulnerable.'

She pressed her hand close into his side. 'Joe's the same,' she said. 'That's why I don't know what it is.'

'But you tell me to look at it,' he said, putting his arm round her.

She grinned at him. 'You're not me.'

And as he pulled her closely against him, she said, 'You can have caviare, Polish duck, Hungarian goulash, Mexican chicken, pickled onions, pilchards, sardines, pickled herrings, smoked oysters' – she got up and looked in the cupboard – 'Indian mango chutney, hot curry, mild curry, peaches, I don't think there's any Christmas pudding left, any sort of soup' – she turned round to face him, crouching at the cupboard by the oven – 'and there're probably other things, if you like. I can't see very well, it's a bit untidy. We've got no money so we have to get everything on Joe's account, and they only sell things in cans; or bottles. And since it caters for the bourgeoisie, it only sells exotic foods; but I think they're nice – don't you? The possums come up to the dump outside and rummage around in the cans; they seem to like it.'

They began with caviare and biscuits flavoured with sesame seed.

'So you don't know what he's been writing about?'

'Yes, I told you: Joe. I sneak a look now and then when they're finished – when he's out or something, you know.'

She came over from the cupboard and poured herself some more wine. The light cast a golden sheen over furrows in her sweater, over her cheeks, so that she looked warm, soft, glowing.

'I wish you wouldn't look like that,' he said.

'Like what?' The sheen rippled as she moved to put the flagon down, and he grabbed her hand and pulled her down to the mattress again.

He said, 'It just wouldn't be a brilliant idea; it's not even that it would upset Joe – '

'Thanks.'

'No, but on principle he probably wouldn't let it. But it would be a betrayal even if it didn't, wouldn't it? Even if he never knew.'

'Sometimes,' she said, 'I wonder if anything could upset Joe, if anything could affect him or get through to him at all. He's almost anaesthetized. He goes from disaster to disaster and just carries on doing the same things. And writes about them. And then goes and does them again. It's as if as long as he can make a story out of it, he doesn't care: it just doesn't affect him, doesn't hurt him or anything. He cares more about his stories than about anyone – even himself. You know, sometimes I think if I could find a way of getting through to him, of hurting him so he'd have to feel something, I'd do it; just to hurt him so he'd feel it. But I can't think of anything.'

She filled up both glasses again.

'Even if I did go to bed with you,' she said, 'I don't think he'd care. He'd just sort of, you know, sort of laugh, and – '

'And write another story.'

'He would. So, I don't know, sometimes I just feel so helpless, so frustrated, you know.'

'So there's no point in sleeping with me?' He said it in a tone of agreement, like a statement that had already been agreed on.

'No,' she said.

'Thanks;' his turn this time.

'Sorry,' she said, 'but you know what I mean.'

She put her glass down and kissed him again, and they lay on the mattress together.

'Look,' she said, 'look, honestly, mostly I don't want to sleep with anyone else anyway. You probably can't understand it but I love him; I just don't want anyone else.'

She pulled him very close while she spoke.

'It's just, oh Graham, it's just so hopeless. I couldn't "betray" him because I don't think there's anything he cares about; I can't do anything; he's not involved with me, all he's involved with is his stories.'

He grinned, sympathetically, for all of them. 'I've just got fewer stories,' he said, 'but I know what he feels.'

And she hugged on to him. While the more he thought about Joe, the more Margot said, the more he wondered why he should care at all about betraying him, why he should even use so absurd a word. That concern on the return from the beach had been merely a terror of Margot, a terror of getting into some absurd relationship with her and Joe. The strength of the recoil from the idea of 'betraying' Joe was a measure, perhaps, of how much he wanted to, how much he should, perhaps, betray him. But having thought about it all again, and considered the difficulties and objections, even if to reject them, raised his doubts. And though he lay beside her kissing her, and her hands stroked all over him, his mind hovered separately, doubtingly.

'But it would be nice,' she said, holding him, pressing him.

'Let's eat first,' he reminded her.

So she stood up sadly. And he was afraid he had now made her annoyed.

She stirred the soup and looked at him – sitting on the mattress and looking at the rough walls, the typewriter on the table, the darkness through the window.

'If you don't want to read the one he's working on, what about the others; the ones he's just finished?'

'Won't he mind?'

'He won't know.'

Outside there was just the darkness, and the rain drumming on the corrugated iron roof, the shafts of rain beating against it and sluicing down the furrows. He stood up to join her to let his hands stroke over her breasts but she wriggled free.

35

'Don't,' she said, shortly, 'because you're not going to do anything so don't just mess around. It only makes me irritable.'

So he went across to Joe's desk.

Before he took out those unsmutched white sheets from their manila folders, before his fingers probed the collection, fumbling along the edges of the pages, easing off paper clips, he knew that Joe would mind. Each story had its own folder, which he spread open, gently bending and pressing it to stay flat, as bees force open the petals of flowers. Sometimes a clip he had not noticed would spring off as he bent back the covers, snapping like a cord breaking. He unclothed the stories, taking them from their covers as if he were prising open oysters. He glanced at their titles and then softly flicked through their pages, flicking at the sheets, unopened since they'd been corrected, flicking sometimes five or six times before catching at an edge that would open for him. He looked through them for their titles and their settings, rapidly yet carefully, his sight washing over words softly, silently, like a quiet sea over shells. His fingers turned the pages gently. He was not rough. They were the same fingers that had stroked Margot's buttocks, that had held off from fondling her nipples. But they did not hold off here. He lay on the mattress, wriggling his hips into a comfortable position, the stories beside him. He was glad, when she called soup, to delay a reading of them. But after the hot soup he lay down again and, taking the topmost of the stories, holding it by its edges as film is held, rested it on the mattress before him.

He read slowly at first to evaluate Joe's development, to establish whether there was any development. He read to see if Joe was on to anything new, in case a new richness had thickened or there had been a blaze of metaphorical efflorescence. The display of Joe's emotional life was only a subsidiary interest. He did not have Margot's investment in that. She asked him if he'd got to the story about Lydia: he wasn't sure except for the finely marked face and the small breasts, he knew nothing about Lydia. Why need he care, as Margot did, about Joe's past life, his past loves, his past betrayals, his current infidelities? 'That bitch in that story, the one he goes over the mountains with,' she called, from the oven: but it wasn't that bitch that interested him, but Joe's lyrical treatment of the mountain trip and the swim in the cool clear sea, their early morning bathing in the sharp translucence. That, and the ending, and the framework he had set the story in that so enhanced it. 'Oh yes,' he agreed when she told him it was Helen, 'she is a bitch.' But it was Joe's new control that he was cursing, the bitch of assurance that was in Joe. 'But don't you think it's a waste of a good story on her?' He hadn't thought of it at all. He didn't see that she had anything to do with the story, but was like one of the drops of clear water beading on her breasts, or the striped pebbles at the sea's edge. That any of them had any existence other than in the story or any gratitude to, let alone claim on Joe, he had never considered. 'Don't you think she's a rat to him at the end?' she said. He wondered how Joe had achieved that ending, with its fine balance, the irresolvable ambivalence of attitude between the two figures, the complexities of involvement and repudi-ation, the final frozen tableau that represented the whole action and like a pedestal supported and sustained it.

But the old flatness was still there. He could find traces of it, of the old over explicitness, the clumsiness: gold amongst the dross, the silt, the rubble. It gave him a sense of comfortable familiarity, an ease. He registered the redundancies, the spelled out endings, the unrealized and untransmuted autobiography, and said nothing. And he said nothing about the new control that Joe's bush exile must have given him; he imagined it was the exile, and not just Margot. Though at the thought he took another drink and looked across at her, licking her fingers with relish for the Polish duck.

'Have you read the one about the abortion?' she said. 'I don't know who it is. Joe won't say. And you can't tell with his crummy stories, you can't ever identify people from them.' She poured out most of the remainder of the flagon. 'I only guessed it was Pat from what he'd told me about her once; when he was pissed of course.' She joined him on the mattress and flicked through the manuscripts for the abortion. Her fingers left grease stains, but she just pulled a face. 'Too bad,' she said, 'he'll just

37

have to type those pages again; or give up being anal about them.' 'I read that one,' he said. 'Did you read the gang bang one?' she asked; and when they'd read that, as well as he could with her interjections and with eating the last of the meal and drinking the wine, she ruffled through the sheets again to find the day his wife walked out. 'And I don't blame her,' she said.

He lay there, sated with duck and soup and caviare, his eyes tired from reading in the poor light, his back burning from the sun. He felt tired now from having spent so long in the sun, in the open air. He rested his head against her breasts and she stroked his hair affectionately. She got up to go and open a tin of camembert that she'd left warming in the oven. She opened a bottle of wine because they had finished the last of the flagon.

He turned on his back and lay looking at the iron roof and the beams supporting it. His head was muzzy with wine and the reading and the sun – swimming, waves breaking and stirring up the sand, muddying it again each time it settled, ceaselessly shifting the particles and blurring their gritty identity to a cloudy suspension. He nibbled at the cheese but he had eaten too much already, sipped at the wine with no great enthusiasm, no great need. He stood up for comfort, for change, to stretch his legs and clear his head. There was no room in which to pace around, so he leant over the typewriter table and leafed through the few pages of the story Joe had begun. He brought them over to the mattress and read them and handed them to Margot, who spilt wine on them, a spreading red stain, when he bumped against her as he stood up again to get the last unfinished page. It ripped as he pulled it out of the typewriter because he had not released the carriage. There wasn't anyway enough of the story there to tell how it was going to develop or whether its features were successful; he started to read the notes for it on the table, but couldn't be bothered to finish them. Between them they completed the rape of the stories.

He lay down on the mattress again, looking dully at the roof and yawning.

'I'll come back to town with you,' she said. 'I don't like staying here alone.' And she shuffled the stories roughly together and stacked the plates on the oven. The cork for the wine had got lost so they left it uncorked as they didn't feel like finishing it. The camembert was thrown outside for the possums.

They didn't have much to say on the drive back. There was nothing to see except the rain that obscured even the stars. He was so tired from the sea air, the sunburn, the wine, the reading, that it was a strain enough to keep his eyes on the road.

He dropped her off in town at a friend of hers and refused coffee. When he got back to his own place, he went straight to bed and flaked.

Reading the Signs

It grew under the apple tree. It got a start because nothing much else ever grew there. We did try potatoes occasionally, but you caught your fork in the tree roots trying to dig them up. So that from the apple tree to the fence at the right was my garden, and from the apple tree to the path at the left was my sister's. She put in rocks and moss and things for the fairies.

It grew there with its stubby wooden stem and its bushy branches of leaves and then this amazing pinkish-purplish bugle of a flower. We let it grow because we had never seen anything like it; even before the flower, it had this presence, this numinousness. But the flower was a clarion of mystery. Then the seedpod formed, green and spiky at first, and then it darkened and became rounded and leathery.

We asked everybody what it was, and no one knew. Even Dad must have accepted some of its mystery, because he never pulled it up. Even though under the apple tree was not productive and even though he didn't believe in stripping off all unplanted vegetation like some of the people in the avenue, the bigger weeds got pulled up and put on the compost heap.

So nobody knew, and we picked the seedpod and kept it in a little fish-paste jar in the kitchen window, sitting in the fish-paste jar like an egg in an eggcup on the windowsill above the sink, among the rubber rings that sealed the fruit we bottled in jars, and the hairpins, and the used razor blades, and countless other things. Sometimes the robin would hop in through the open window and peck around. Year after year the windowsill was in the robin's territory.

The seedpod cracked open, and we kept the dark-brown seeds in the bottom of the fish-paste jar through the winter, and they stayed on the windowsill with all the other accreted things and got forgotten. The plant died beneath the apple tree, and the dried stem was tossed onto a bonfire.

The next year, it came again. But the next year it had come all over the rest of England, too. Neighbours had them. The newspapers reported its mysterious appearance throughout the country. The Californian thorn apple, they called it. Jimsonweed. *Datura stramonium.* Said to be deadly poisonous.

'Wonder you didn't poison the lot of us,' Dad said. Poisonous, they all said. No one said it was a hallucinogen. But they stamped them out and burned them just the same.

Once the plant was everywhere and had been named, we didn't know what else to do. We knew there was a mystery, but the naming and the reported spread of it were made to do service for the revelation. We never did take any of it, boiled or brewed or powdered or smoked or rubbed into the skin. The newspapers never suggested you could do that. That sort of knowledge hadn't survived. It was about this time Mum had her fortune read at the village fête and was told that in a few years time she'd be doing the same herself: reading fortunes. She was always able to read the signs. If she dropped a big knife it would be a tall visitor coming, and a little knife a short visitor. The magpies would fly over the fields, one for sorrow, two for joy. But the uses of the thorn apple had been stamped out in the witch burnings. Everything comes in threes was another of Mum's sayings. But the third year the thorn apple didn't come back. And the seeds had got thrown on the fire because of everyone's saying how poisonous it was. I think that was a mistake, not keeping the seeds.

'That flying saucer you saw,' I asked Mum.

'Oh, Michael, did we?' she says. 'I can't remember now.'

It was like this when I needed my precise time of birth for the astrological chart. 'Here we are. Five. One. Or was that the date? Wait until I find my specs.'

'When we were living up the avenue. You remember.'

The avenue was a row of twenty-seven houses, with fields in front of us – because they hadn't built on the other side of the road – and fields behind. They stopped building when the war started. The prisoners of war used to hoe in the fields at the back.

'We were in the back garden talking one evening and it just came across,' Mum said. 'I can't remember if it was our back garden, even.'

'And it just came over the garden?'

'I think so,' Mum said. 'It wasn't very high. It was just like a bright light. It had a sort of tail, I think.'

'And where did it go?'

'It just vanished. It just went. It wasn't there any more.'

'No,' said Dad. 'No, no, no, it was in the front of the houses. We were standing in the road. It was going up the river. It was a meteorite. It was going up the river.'

'What, following it along?'

'That's what it looked like.'

Dad wrote to the paper. 'As an iron-moulder, it seemed to me like a glowing red ball of molten iron.'

Sometimes he would be at home with burns on his hands or feet from molten iron that had spilled. Now he is at home dying of emphysema from the foundry dust.

'It was just like the molten iron when it comes out of the furnace.'

Mum was furious, embarrassed. She went red.

'I never expected them to print it,' Dad said. 'I just wrote it as information for them.'

Other people in town had sighted it. There were other letters.

'You might have known they'd print it.'

'No, I didn't, so that's that,' said Dad.

Mum was mortified. On the forms at school we wrote 'Engineer', not 'Iron-moulder'. Filling in the forms for university, I went off to a private place and my stomach wrenched for a long time and for 'Father's Profession or Occupation' I crossed out 'Profession' and wrote 'Iron-moulder'.

The man at the appointments board, just before I left, congratulated me. 'Well, well,' he said, 'you're tipped for a first, you edited the university paper, you've done very well for an iron-moulder's son.'

Dad said, 'It went along up the river glowing like molten iron and then it exploded. It was a meteorite.'

'There wasn't any noise,' Mum said.

'I didn't say there was any noise,' Dad said. 'It exploded in a big flash.'

'But explosions usually make a noise,' Mum said.

I don't know whether Dad clipped the letter or not. I've had letters in print that were not intended for print. I think I kept them but kept them beneath dark stacks of things.

'People who've seen them don't seem to talk about them much,' I said.

'That's right,' Mum said. 'We didn't talk about it much, did we?' she said to Dad.

What they talked about was the letter. The shame of being a manual worker and the ridicule for having seen a flying saucer and the breaking of the taboo in revealing these things in print.

The Girl Behind the Bar
is Reading Jack Kerouac

The girl behind the bar is reading Jack Kerouac. I find this an omen so I talk to her about Jack Kerouac. The conversation is interrupted as she pours beers. But generally she returns to continue it.

I ask her what time she gets off work. She says she never gets off work. She is a writer. A writer's work is never done.

She needs someone to look over her stories. She needs advice on the markets. We go back to her place to look over her stories. We lie on the bed side by side, turning the pages.

The first story I read is about a girl working in a bar and being picked up by a man. It seems to be developing interestingly. He says he's sure she's got talent and if she comes back to his place with some of her stories he'll make her a star.

She takes it out of my hands and dumps it on the floor.

'He was a jerk,' she says.

I start another one about a girl working in a bar and being picked up by a Scandinavian. They screw for a few pages. She visits him one day when his other girlfriend is there. He tells the other girlfriend this is just a writer who roams around visiting people, nothing sexual, and the other girlfriend believes him. When he meets the girl in the bar again he expects her to be furious; but she is delighted, she has been accepted as a writer.

'I like that one,' I say.

'Do you really?' she says. 'Really? What do you like about it?'

'I like the idea of it,' I say. 'It's nice and ironical. And sexy too. The screwing's very erotic. It's hard to do that well.'

'It's not really hard,' she said, standing up and tugging her shirt over her head and stepping out of her skirt.

'We used to do it like this,' she said, undressing me and screwing me.

'Let's read this one now,' she said; 'this one's quite different.'

It was about a girl who went to a seminar on writing and got off with the seminar panel, a different panellist after every session. The story related their different screwing patterns to their different writing styles. I read the whole story through first to get the general picture, then we went back to the beginning and had a screw every time she made it with a new panellist.

'Is there some coffee or something?' I asked, when we'd gone right through it.

'There's some in the coffee pot ready if you want,' she said. 'What do you want to read next?'

'I thought maybe we could just have some coffee for a while. Like a sort of interlude.'

She put her hand round the back of my neck and twisted my head round to read the next story.

But that was really by way of a joke. She was basically considerate. The story she chose was about a girl who was so committed to her writing she never had time to go around picking up men. But at the same time she had this immense sex drive. She made it with bananas and coke bottles and chocolate bars and such like.

'I'll show you,' she said, getting a banana from the fruit bowl.

'I like that,' I said, sipping my coffee. 'I'm not sure it's great art but I like it. You've got to have different stories for different moods. Maybe it is great art.'

The next was about a jaded writer who could only get a hard on after watching someone make it with bananas, coke bottles, chocolate bars and such like.

She smiled at me and pulled me into her.

After that it was time for her to go to work again. She had a shower while I sat on a stool in the bathroom and read through another story, glancing up at her as I turned the pages. Then she dressed and left. 'Here,' she said before she went out of the door, 'amuse yourself with this one while I'm gone.'

It was about how this man that kept coming into the pub where this girl worked and kept talking about writing and eyeing off her tits so one day she took him back to her place and showed him her stories and they re-enacted the fucks in them all afternoon till she had to go back to work. Then he watched her shower and put her shirt and skirt back on and rush away and then he thought about how she was standing there in the bar being watched by all these men looking at her tits and cunt, and his semen all trickling around in her cunt as they watched her there and he got himself so turned on by thinking about it all he spent the rest of the time she was away playing with himself and pulling himself off till he fell asleep.

'Have a good time?' she asked when she got back in, switching on the bedroom light and taking off her clothes.

The West Midland Underground

The West Midland Underground goes from   to
Or should I say went? Should I have said went? Should I be
saying went? Or even will go. May go. Could go. Could have
gone. Was to have gone. Is to go. Is to have gone? Is it possible to
say is to have gone? Are there certain tenses that do not exist, may
not, cannot, will not, did not; though now do? Perhaps the
impossible tenses are needed for the impossible underground.
Perhaps the hitherto impossible tense will bring into being the
hitherto impossible West Midland Underground.

Henry James: Papau New Guinea has everything you could ever
need. A brief example from a Papuan language of average com-
plexity, Gadsup of the East New Guinea Highlands Phylum, may
be given here to show the structure of the verbs occurring at the
end of sentence – these are simpler verbal forms than the so-
called medial forms. These sentence-final verb forms consist of a
verb stem plus a number of elements suffixed to it. All these,
linked together in a single long word, constitute the sentence-
final verb forms, and such a verb form will show the following
composition: verb stem + benefactor marker (that is, the action is
carried out for the benefit of somebody) + potential marker +
ability marker + statement marker + interrogative marker +
completion marker + subject marker + two emphasis markers
(i.e. kùmù-ánk-àdád-òn-ték-áp-ón-ì-nó-bé) . . . Thus the full
shades of meaning of this elaborate verb form given above can
be expressed in English only inadequately and may best be
rendered by a sentence like 'had he indeed wanted to go down
for him?'

Had she indeed wanted to go down for them? The nun. I recur

remorselessly to the nun's tunnel. Like a movie of memory and compulsion, cutting back and back to those same frames. In the Gaumont, Worcester, I see *The Private Life of Sherlock Holmes* and *Underground*. *Underground* is about an officer parachuted behind the German lines who works with the Maquis, shoots people, blows up bridges. Our truer underground runs still beneath. Sometimes buildings would collapse along the high street, and we always believed they fell into the nun's tunnel.

> She trailed along behind the others as they returned along the underground corridor from the cathedral. At least having Mass there once a week was a change from the other six days when it was held in the nunnery. A change – but to what effect? She suddenly realized in all fullness how barren her life was, when she could call the difference between pious faces in the priory and the same pious faces in the cathedral a change.
>
> She jumped up suddenly. All the stored up misery had burst out, overwhelmed her. But she had sat there crying for too long. The door at the end of the passage would be closed, barred, bolted. She ran. She ran through the blackness of the corridor, on, on.

In 1959 I was writing about the nun's tunnel in the school magazine. In 1972 I add her into the story about cats in London. Why do I return to the nun's tunnel? The door was bolted. She died in the tunnel between the cathedral and the nunnery and her ghost still walks.

Was that the West Midland Underground? Does the West Midland Underground, alone of all undergrounds, have a ghost to parade along it? The White Lady of Worcester, patron saint of the underground. We could make a million, casting medallions of her for every freak's neck.

As for the dimensions, they are no more certain than the tenses.

Does		historically	
Did		topographically	
Will	the West Midland	geographically	
May	Underground go	bibliographically	from
Can		chronologically	
Should		adjectivally	

the Anglo-Saxons		the Industrial Revolution
hills		valleys
limestone	to	marl
Feckenham		Wyre Piddle
1100hrs		2300hrs
bad		worse

Where would we look for direction?

During the war the signposts were all taken down so parachuted spies wouldn't be able to find their way around. The
land was without identity. When had the signposts first been
put up, when had the land first been named for those who did
not know the names? For those who grew from it, the names
were always there, each lane and hill, track and cluster of
buildings. With merely an odd milestone for the aspirant Dick
Whittingtons. And then came the century that broke the sec-
recies, that labelled the intimacies for anyone to see. The mys-
teries were revealed and the strangers spread over the land.

But with the war the labels and arrows were all erased; the
surfaces were cleansed, and places existed only in themselves,
their names accessible only for those who were at them, not for
those who would only point. Perhaps it was then that the
arrows to the W. Midland Underground were removed. And
after the war, never re-erected. Perhaps they had got mislaid.
Perhaps the men who had pulled down the signs had died, or
lost their memories, and nothing had been written down for fear
the enemy might gain access to the records. So that there was
nothing from which to rediscover the underground. Yet archae-
ologists could find traces of the old post holes if they looked.
Though could they deduce the direction of the arrows from the

49

post holes? The station entrances must lie there for discovery, beneath their thickets of brambles, their landslides of shale. Moles and ferrets and dormice scuttling into hiding there, bats hanging from the tunnel roofs to issue out at twilight.

Another possibility is that of deliberate closure by the overground; as with the canals. In my days of searching through the countryside I stalked the clues of this other possibility. I often crossed the canal, which canal it needs no more to answer than to question, exquisite brevity. And on the soft worn red brick bridges overarching the dried up canal bed were rusted iron plaques, asserting ownership by the London and West Midland, or some such combination, steam locomotive company, taking us back to those days when the overground had bought the canal companies to close down their cheap competition. And could it be that the overground had bought out too the underground, and affixed iron plaques of ownership to stations and arches and tunnels and platforms; and closed it down. And as the canals silted up and the lock gates rotted and crumbled and the reeds took over, resuming the deep cut of the navvies back to the contours of the brambly hills, unseen, the tunnels collapsed behind their boarded entrances, the air chimneys piercing up through the hills were fenced off and bricked over and the briars and hawthorn spread across them, and within the bricks fell from the lining one by one, as tree roots and incautious moles pushed and encountered no resistance. The underground filled with the hollow bones of small animals and stale air; the heavy drapes of cobwebs closed off the passages that had fallen into disuse. While the overground roared above crushing the bed of granite chips beneath its steel tracks and creosoted sleepers.

RESEARCH SERVICE BIBLIOGRAPHIES / Series 4, no. 61 / Underground radio communication / Compiled by I. Boleszny / Adelaide. / Public Library of South Australia / January 1966. /

At last our network of underground radio communication spreads the counter culture through our global ether, underground nomadic transmitter caravans sending out new writing and revolution on accessible frequencies at the underground hours. What k/Ms will find them, what is the West Midland Underground Transmitter's call signal? 'Articles prefixed by x are to the best of our knowledge not available in South Australia. Photocopies of these references can usually be obtained from libraries in other states and overseas. While this may sometimes be expensive, we have found that on most occasions the cost is about 2/– (20 cents) per page.'

1963
    3 X Funktechnik und Elektroakustik sowie Sonderanlagen der Drahtnachrichtentechnik im Bergbau . . . H. Jahn. BERGBAUTECHNIK 13:82–91, February 1963; 13:131–45, March 1963.
    4   New transducers for communicating by seismic waves. il diag K. Ikrath *and* W. Schneider. ELECTRONICS 36:51–5, 12 April 1963.
    5   Investigation of the design of underground communication systems. L.M. Valles *and others*. IEEE INTERNATIONAL CONVENTION RECORD 11, pt.8: 234–41, 1963.
    6   Modes in lossy stratified media with application to underground propagation of radio waves. M.E. Viggh. IEEE TRANSACTIONS ON ANTENNAS AND PROPAGATION AP–11:318–23, May 1963.
    7 X Electronic equipment for mine communications. R.E. Havener. MECHANIZATION 27:52–4, March 1963.
    8   Communications in mining industry. R. Lee. MINING JOURNAL 261:30–3, 12 July 1963.

From about three a.m. there isn't much happening on the cab radio, we'll broadcast stories then. They'll be picked up by every cab operating. When the service gets known people will start taking cabs in order to hear the stories. Then we can extend to other times; eventually we'll broadcast twenty-four hours a day; we can have breaks for commercials, we can stop the story and give the cab calls, Bondi Road, Bondi to Darling Street Balmain,

Newcastle Hotel, George Street to St Vincent's Hospital; and then back to the story. We can even fit the messages into the story; we have people phoning a cab in the story and we hear the operator calling the cab for them and when they're in the cab they listen idly to the cab radio calling Steyne Hotel, Manly to Sylvania Hotel, Sylvania and so on, and they listen idly to the cab radio as long as there are messages to be transmitted; and if there aren't any messages to be transmitted they can be written into the story to create cab bookings. In the end the entire population of the city would be taking cabs in order to hear the stories. Different companies will run different programmes. It will be impossible to get a cab to travel in; people will be going into bookshops to buy short story collections in order to travel home. 'Have you got the volume of short stories *Seaforth Crescent, Seaforth to Mort Street, Balmain?*' 'This is the last one, sir.' 'Do I get a ten per cent discount as a university teacher?' 'Not on paperbacks under a total of twenty-three miles, sir.' The biggest boom in the short story known to history will eventuate. The presses will be pouring volumes out, daily newspapers featuring them, special stories printed on cornflakes packets and passiona bottles; fragments of stories: 'Collect the entire story from the ends of ten packets of meat pies.' New visitors to the city will have to discover the dead hour, in between the afternoon and evening story shifts; it will be as impossible to buy a short story between three and four p.m. as in the past it had been to travel by cab.

Gadsup was at college with me before he joined the East New Guinea Highlands Phylum. Even as an undergraduate, without the range of verbal forms that later was indeed to have become his, he had a knack of memorable expression. I remember one vacation entering The Cellars, a basement coffee lounge in which the youth of the West Midlands gathered in their motorcycling jackets and tattoos.

'I say,' he said as we sipped our coffee, his voice reverberating through the underground rooms, 'don't these marble-topped tables remind you of altars in a Greek temple, Diana at Ephesus or something?'

In the cellars the youth of the W. Midlands sat and looked.
'Just waiting for a human sacrifice.'
The coffee very hot.

Likewise he once boomed out, entering a country pub, 'I'm thinking of writing a novel about someone who turns to Catholicism from excessive masturbation.'

The 'excessive' was a note characteristic of Gadsup, the shade of meaning he strode unerringly towards.

I wouldn't think the Salwarpe has trout. Don't trout streams have to be through limestone or something? Clear water? The Salwarpe wasn't clear; but ran slowly and muddily through clay, sandstone, trundled along. I used to canoe up it and that took about eight times as long as just walking because it meandered so much. It didn't really want to get to the Severn and lose its identity. So it kept winding from side to side. And didn't flow too fast. And then all the way along were these mills, that had been there for centuries, damming up its hardly forceful flow, and letting what wasn't dammed up rush away through some narrow hurtling mill race, which as soon as it got round past the mill settled into the old comfortable sluggishness. Hawford Mill, Bill's Mill, Porter's Mill. Porter put up Queen Elizabeth when she went through, at one of his houses. I don't know who Bill was. But none of the mills works now; they just dam up water and the soft drink bottles and the twigs and the old boots, and let some of the other water hurtle down the mill race, which it probably likes doing, once in a while.

And then alongside the Salwarpe is the Wych canal; straight as a die. They ran together like two cops or two comedians, the straight one and the funny one, the nice one and the heavy one. There's a fable in it too, sermons in stones and something in running brooks. Well, the canal isn't running any more. Back in the end of the eighteenth century it was Brindley's most beautiful canal, he said it was, and it ran as straight as a die from the Severn to Droitwich, to take the salt away. And all the way it ran straight, the Salwarpe wriggled along beside it, making all these sinuous, concertina'd curves, like Marilyn Monroe alongside

John Wayne. But then there wasn't too much use for the straight canal and it silted up; there wasn't too much use for the winding Salwarpe either, but it had always been there and had its own sources of water and current and so just kept on flowing not worrying any too much about use.

But just on the offchance of trout I thought it might lead to the underground so I walked along, not exactly beside it since in that rainy winter everything had become pretty waterlogged, and between the old canal and the river, often a distance of only three or four yards or so, it tended to get a bit swampy; but I walked near it, along roads and paths that crossed over it or ran beside it and crossed back over it again. Till I came to this bare cleared patch of ground, and this high wire fence, and these new concrete buildings, and a label: Ladywood Pollution Control Unit. And down below the Ladywood Pollution Control Unit ran the Salwarpe. Maybe the West Midland Underground is a Dostoievskian underground.

The Salwarpe may have outlived John Wayne but technology gets its revenge in the end. Now they pour shit on the river I used to canoe along. And for certain there wouldn't be any trout there. And as the winter went on men with tractors and power saws went along the winding curling organic edge of the Salwarpe and cut down all the willows that hung over it, all the hawthorn and elder and bramble that ran down from the bank to the water's edge; they cut away everything that might ever collapse and hold up the flow of shit into the Severn. They razed the edges of the Salwarpe flat like an airfield. Because if an old willow tree that had grown on the edge there for fishermen to sit under and kingfishers to fish under and mayflies to mill beneath, decided to lay itself down in the river that had undermined its roots all its years, decided just to surrender itself to the flow, then it would hold up all the shit, and they had to get the shit from the Ladywood Pollution Control Centre as quickly as ever possible into the Severn where it would be washed down with the fuller flow and eventually out to the Bristol Channel and America.

I guess the next they'll cut off all the corners of the old meandering Salwarpe which Brindley would've done if he could've done only he didn't have the technology but he thought of it, so the shit will just shoot down straight into the Severn without having to wind round at all; and then they'll concrete the whole top of the river over, with semi-circular pre-cast concrete culverts, and pump through double the volume; then they'll concrete over the Severn. Every river in the country will be arched over with pre-cast concrete culverts, arteries of shit being pumped along the old waterways, to form a solid, coagulate ring round the British Isles.

What are the advantages of looking for the West Midland Underground?

1 Health; daily walks through the clear air, good for the circulation, leg muscles, lungs, digestion.
2 Mental ease; the state of mental relaxation induced by walking through the country lanes, numbness.
3 Architectural; to explore the varieties of half-timbering, the black and white domestic architecture of the district. There is a barn built of stone, rare in this district, which a countryman who lives in the cruck cottage next to it said was stone left over from the church. That would be round about five hundred years ago. The corrugated iron roof was added later.
4 Historical; Warwick the Kingmaker was born in a half-timbered huge manor house beside the Salwarpe. On the skyline you can see Woodbury Hill where Caractacus made his famous last stand against the Roman invader.
5 Geographical; the way hills roll and rivers wind.
6 Botanical; flowers and plants and things, most of them not in flower yet. I can only tell their names when they're in flower.
7 Natural fauna; dormice, water rats, moles, but they stay underground and you can only see the mole hills; there are badgers underground too, I know where a badger set is, tunnelling into a ridge beside the old canal. Perhaps the fauna are there before us.

8 To talk to oneself watched only by cattle.

9 Fantasy. A long straight road, must be a Roman road running to Droitwich to get salt. Flat fields each side. Distantly, the clip clop of a horse. I walk, my breath white in the cold air. I am a dragon and behind a gentle knight is pricking on the plain. A lady with a headscarf, riding jacket, jodhpurs; she turns to smile down on me, I turn to smile up to her, we wish each other good day. She rides on, along the straight road between the flat fields. She rides out of sight. At the crossroads I look for horseshoe marks in the mud at the roadside. There are horseshoe marks in all the mud, at every roadside, in every direction. For weeks I walk along the old Roman road, salt free, lady less.

10 Hope. Somewhere, over the rainbow, the crock of gold, the gates of Eden, the doors of bliss.

The Man of Slow Feeling

After the accident he lay for weeks in the still white ward. They fed him intravenously but scarcely expected him to live. Yet he did live, and when at last they removed the bandages from his eyes, it was found he could see. They controlled what he could see carefully, keeping the room dimmed, the blinds down, at first; but gradually increased his exposure to light, to the world around. Slowly his speech came back. He blocked for some time on words he could not remember, could no longer enunciate; but gradually his vocabulary returned. But he had lost sensation, it seemed. He could not smell the flowers Maria brought into the small private ward. And when she gave him the velvety globed petals to touch, he could not feel them. All foods were the same to him. The grapes she mechanically bought, he could only see. They had neither touch nor taste for him. If he shut his eyes and returned to darkness again, he did not know what he was eating. Yet he was not totally without sensation – it was not as if he was weightless or bodiless. He was conscious of lying in bed day after day, his body lying along the bed – perhaps because the constant pressure reached through to his numbed nerves. But the touch of Maria's fingers on his cheeks, the kiss of her lips against his, he could not feel, nor mouth the taste of her.

And yet as he lay alone in that small white room odd sensations came to him, brushed him with their dying wings. As if, lying there with only his thoughts and imaginings, he could conjure back the taste of grapes, the soft touch of Maria's hand, the searching pressure of her kiss. They surprised him, these sensations; often they would make him wake from a slight sleep as if a delightful dream had achieved an actuality: but when he awoke he was always totally alone, and remembered nothing of any dream. It was often, as he lay there, as if someone had actually touched him, or forced grapes against his palate, and he would want to cry out at the unexpectedness of it. If imagination, it could only have been triggered by the workings of his subconscious. He mentioned it to the nurses, and they said that it could be that he was getting his sensations back. He did not argue with them, pointing out that there were no correlatives to the sensations, no objects provoking them. It was like a man feeling pain in a foot already amputated: a foot he would not be getting back. The sensations were the ghosts of feelings he had once had, nerve memories of a lost past.

Released from hospital, Maria took him back to the house in the country. They made love that first night, but he could not feel her full breasts, her smooth skin, and making love to her was totally without sensation for him. Its only pleasures were voyeuristic and nostalgic: his eyes and ears allowed him to remember past times – like seeing a sexual encounter at the cinema. The thought came to him that the best way to get anything from sex now was to cover the walls and ceilings with mirrors, so that at least he could have a full visual satisfaction to replace his missing senses. But he said nothing to Maria. He said nothing, but he knew she realized that for him it was now quite hopeless.

He was woken in the night by a dream of intercourse, the excitement of fondling a body, the huge relief of orgasm. He lay awake, the vividness of it reminding him bitterly of what was now lost to him.

The early days back in the house he found disorienting. Within the white walls confining the ward experience had been limited for him; he saw little, encountered little; the disturbing nerve memories were few. But released, now they swelled to a riot, as if exposure to the open world had revived dormant, dying memories for their final throes. Released, his body was a continual flux of various sensation, of smell, of taste, of touch; yet still with no sensations from his experiences. He could walk beside the dung heap at the field's corner, ready to manure the land, and though he inhaled deeply hoping its pungency would break through his numbness, he could experience nothing. When Maria was not looking, he reached his hand into the dung: he felt nothing. A visual repugnance, but no physical sensation, no recoil of nausea.

Yet at tea suddenly the full pungency of the foul dung swept across to him, his hand unfeelingly holding a meringue was swamped in the heavy foul stickiness of the dung. He left the table, walked across to the window that looked out onto the wide lawns. There was nothing outside to provoke his sensations; and if there had been how could his touch have been affected from outside? His touch and smell had not, as he'd momentarily hoped, returned. Maria asked what was the matter, but he said nothing. He went to the bathroom, but oddly did not feel nausea. He expected to, biting that momentarily dung drenched meringue. But his stomach recorded no sensations. His intellect's interpretation had misled him; his mind was interpreting a nausea he would have felt, in his past life, an existence no longer his.

Yet in bed as he reached out to fondle, hopelessly, Maria who made love with him now more eagerly, more readily, more desperately, uselessly, pointlessly than ever before, his stomach was gripped by a sudden retching nausea, and he had to rush to the bathroom to vomit.

'My poor dear,' said Maria, 'oh my poor dear.'

He wondered whether he should rest again, to recover the placidity he had known in the hospital. But to rest in bed, although he could read or hear music, meant his life was so reduced. At least to walk round the fields or into the village gave him stimulation for those senses that remained.

But activity seemed disturbing. And provoked a riot of these sense memories, these million twitching amputated feet.

Then, one day, he realized his senses were not dead.

It was a compound realization, not a sudden epiphany. In the morning he had driven the car and going too fast over the humpbacked bridge that crossed the canal, had provoked a scream from Maria. He had asked in alarm what was the matter.

THE MAN OF SLOW FEELING

'Nothing,' she said, 'it's just that it took the bottom out of my stomach, going over the bridge like that.'

'I'm sorry,' he said, 'I didn't realize I was going that fast. I can't feel that sort of thing now.'

Indeed he had forgotten, till she reminded him, that the sensation existed.

They made love at noon, not because he could experience anything, but because in his dreams and in his waking nerve memories, he so often re-experienced the ecstasy in actuality denied him. He perhaps half hoped to recapture the experience. But never did.

Maria got up to cook lunch, absurdly spending great labour on foods he could not taste, perhaps hoping to lure his taste from its grave. She rushed from the kitchen to his bed when he gave a sudden cry. But he was laughing when she reached the bedroom.

'Sorry,' he said. 'It's just like you said, your stomach dropped out going over the bridge, and that must have reminded me of it. It just happened this minute, lying here.'

She touched his brow with her cool hand, whose coolness and presence he could not feel. He brushed her away, irritated by her solicitude. As he ate his lunch, he brooded over his cry of alarm. And later, buying cigarettes in the village shop, for the nervous habit he realized that had always caused him to smoke, not the taste, he came on the truth as his body was suffused with the sudden aliveness of intercourse, the convulsive ecstasy of orgasm.

'Are you all right, sir?' the shopkeeper asked.

'I'm fine, fine,' he said. 'It's it's' (it's nothing he was about to say mechanically, but it was ecstasy); 'it's quite all right,' he said.

Walking back, he was elated at realizing sensation was not denied him, but delayed. He looked at his watch and predicted he would taste his lunch at four o'clock. And sitting on the stile at the field corner, he did. In excitement he ran, his meal finished, to tell Maria, to tell her ecstatically that the accident had not robbed him of sensation, but dulled and slowed its

60

passage along his nerves. When he tripped on a log and grazed his knee without any feeling, he knew, ambivalently, that in three hours the pain would be registered; he waited in excitement for confirmation of his prediction, in anxiety about the pain it would bring.

But his knowledge was a doubtful advantage. The confusions of senses had been disturbing, but not worrying. It was the prediction now that tore him with anxiety. Cutting his finger while sharpening a pencil, he waited tense for the delayed pain; and even though cutting his finger was the slightest of hurts, it filled three hours of anxiety. He worked out with Maria that the well-timed cooking of food could appetize his tasteless smelless later meal; but few meals could produce rich smells three hours before serving. He could not do anything the slightest nauseating, like cleaning drains or gutting chickens, for fear of the context in which his senses would later register and produce in their further three hours the possibility of his vomiting. Defecation became nightmarish, could ruin any ill-timed meal, or intercourse. And ill-timed intercourse would ruin any casual urination. He toyed with the idea of keeping a log book, so that by consulting what happened three hours back, he knew what he was about to feel. He experimented one morning, and in a sort of way it worked. For he spent so long noting down each detail in his book, he had little time to experience anything. He realized how full life is of sensations, as hopelessly he tried to record them all.

He developed a device, instead, consisting primarily of a small tape-recorder which he carried always with him. He spoke a constant commentary into it of his sensate actions and, through earphones, his commentary would be played back to him after a three hours delay, to warn him of what he was about to feel. The initial three hours, as he paced the fields, were comparatively simple, though he worried at the limitations it would impose on his life and experience, having to comment on it in its entirety, each trivial stumble, each slight contact. But after three hours had passed, and his bruised slow nerves were transmitting his sensations, the playback came in. And he found he could not both record his current activities in a constant flow, and hear a constant commentary on his three hours back activities, momentarily prior to his sensations of those past ones. He braced himself for the predicted sensation that his recorded voice warned him of, and in doing so forgot to maintain his current commentary for his three hours hence instruction. And maintaining his commentary, he forgot to act on the playback and lost the value of its warnings. And recurring again to it, intent on gaining from its predictions, he began to follow its record as instructions, and when he caught the word 'stumble' from his disembodied voice, he stumbled in obedience, forgetting to hold himself still for the sensation of stumbling. And what, anyway, warned of a stumble, was he to do? Sit passively for the experience to flow through him and pass? What he had recorded as advice seemed peremptory instruction, terse orders that his nerves responded to independent of his volition. The playback possessed an awful authority, as if the voice were no longer his, and the announced experiences (which he had never felt) foreign to him: and at each random whim of the voice, distorted parodically from his own, his sensations would have inevitably to respond. And he the mere frame, the theatre for the puppet strings to be hung and tugged in.

He could never coordinate commentary and playback: the one perpetually blocked the other, as he tried to hear one thing and say another. And he would confuse them and having spoken a sensation into the microphone before him would immediately prepare to experience it, forgetting the delay that had to come. His sensations became as random to him as before in that maze of playback and commentary and memory. And when he did accidently, reflectively, re-enact the activity his playback warned him to prepare for, then he had to record another warning of that activity for his three hours later sensation: and it was as if he were to be trapped in a perpetual round to the same single repeated stumble.

He abandoned notebooks and tape-recorders. He sat at the window awaiting his sensations. Sex became a nightmare for him, its insensate action and empty voyeurism bringing only the cerebral excitement of a girlie magazine, its consequence a wet dream, the tension of waiting for which (sometimes with an urgent hope, sometimes with the resistant wished-against tension) would agonize him – keep him sleepless or, in the mornings, unable to read or move. And the continual anxiety affected his whole sexual activity, made him ejaculate too soon, or not at all; and he had to wait three hours for his failures to reach him, knowing his failure, reminded of it cruelly three hours after his cerebral realization.

He could not sleep. Any activity three hours before sleep, would awaken him, bumping into a door, drinking wine, switching off a record player. The sensations would arouse his tense consciousness. He tried to control against this, spending the three hours before sleep in total stillness and peace, but the tension of this created its own anxiety, produced psychosomatic pains: of which he would be unaware until they woke him.

He thought back with a sort of longing to his hospital bed, when without stimulation he had experienced only the slightest of sensations. But in those bare walls of the bare room, he might almost have been in a tomb. If life were only bearable without sensation, what was the life worth that he could bear?

Maria came back from town one day to find him dead in the white, still bathroom. He had cut his arteries in a bath in the Roman way, the hot water, now rich vermilioned, to reduce the pain of dying. Though, she told herself, he would not have felt anything anyway, he had no sensation.

But three hours afterwards, what might he have felt?

Hector and Freddie

Hector would always tell the story of how he met Freddie to anyone who would listen. Everything Hector told was 'the story of'. Freddie would interject, 'No,' 'No,' half laughing in unbelieving embarrassment that Hector would create such travesties. 'No, it's not true at all. I don't know what makes you say such things.'

'Oh shut up, Freddie,' Hector would say, drawing out the -dee of Freddie; and then, to the auditor, 'it's just because he's modest, see.'

It's just because he's Welsh he always says see, see.

Freddie had been very lonely in those days, his first weeks at Oxford. 'He never spoke to anyone in hall, just sat there, see, huddled up in his gown, a great enwrapping scholarly one, his eyes just peering out above the folds, like he was in purdah. We used to watch him, peering over the bread bowls, slyly.'

'They didn't have bread bowls,' Freddie would interject.

'Doesn't matter man, don't be so bloody literal minded. At nights he would go back to his rooms alone, along the still, echoing corridors, his little footsteps going pat, pat, pat, alone. Then he would draw his curtains and undress by the red glow of his electric heater, divesting each garment in a sort of dance, slowly, ritualistically. It was like a private strip show.'

'How can you say all this, Hector? It's just not true, you weren't even there.'

'But there were unblocked keyholes; and rooms to rent across the road that looked in.'

'But the curtains were drawn.'

'Not close enough, though, Freddie. You never pulled them right tight.' And returned to his theme he would continue. 'So he would undress slowly, luxuriatingly, stretching out his arms

and dropping his tie, his shirt, his vest, in little heaps around the
room. Have you ever noticed, he's got very graceful movements,
a sort of natural grace? Go on Freddie, let them see you move.
Stand up now and walk around, let them see. It's not like
walking, see, but a sort of undulation – gentle lapping waves of
movement. Go on, Freddie, show them.'

Freddie would take off his glasses and bend over to clean them
with his handkerchief, to wipe away the mist from them, to veil
his blushes.

'Then he would take off his shoes, his socks, one at a time,
slowly, gently, stroking his feet, caressing his limbs as their
nakedness was exposed; then his belt, whirling it round like a
lariat and leaping in the air, up and down, up and down, whirling
his belt all the time, as his trousers slowly fell, slowly slid down
his lithe thighs, over his knees, rustling down to his ankles in little
folds, and then he would give one huge leap and spring right out
of them. He never wears underpants. He's so lithe, so physical.'

'Fuck off, Hector,' he would say, myopically protected from
the visitors like the gentle ostrich, smudging his glasses furiously
with dandruff stained fingers he had rubbed into his hair, the
obscenity a desperate and unconvincing gesture at bravery,
which he knew Hector would never take offence at.

'Then he would get into bed. It was a big wide bed, and he
would talk to himself in it. Outside in the corridor you could hear
him. He'd hold dialogues. He'd lie on one side of the bed and say
something, ask himself a question; then he would turn over, roll
to the other side of the bed and answer himself. He'd have great
long discussions, rolling from side to side of the bed. Sometimes
he'd use different voices, like he was stereophonic. Treble and
bass, answering each other. It could be very beautiful, strophe
and antistrophe.'

STREPHON   These mountaines witness shall, so shall these
           vallies,
KLAIUS   These forrests eke, made wretched by our
           musique,
STREPHON   Our morning hymn is this,
KLAIUS   and song at evening.

'One night he was squatting naked by his fire, his clothes shed like raped corpses in a charnel house, when, howling up the stairs – '

'It's just not true. I'd had a bath and was drying myself by the fire.'

' – glowing celestial rosie red, love's proper hue, incredibly sexy, crouched there, like a virgin on Diana's altar – '

'What for chrissake do you know about Diana's altar, Hector?'

'Things I could never dare reveal to you, Freddie.'

Crouched there, then, in the darkened room, the only light that from the electric heater's red glow, naked, he heard the pulse of feet up the stairs, racing along the corridor, doors opening and slamming shut, and a voice shouting; and as the steps pounded onwards, coming closer, the voice, the words, the reiterated phrase became distinct.

'You have nothing to lose except your trousers.'

Freddie heard the drunk swing open the door of Hector's room and call out his slogan, slam it shut, and then, inexorably, approach, seize, rend open the protection of his own enclosing darkness:

'You have nothing to lose except your trousers,' he roared hoarsely, breathlessly, and then focused on the naked figure crouched there in the soft firelight.

His laughter ricocheted along the stepped and winding passage, poured down the stone stairwells in sobbing torrents, howls of gulping mirth slowly passing, winding away in a long and slow diminuendo through the shattered night.

Hector came from his room and walked to Freddie's open door.

'Oh my God,' he said.

And Freddie hugged himself closer, his knees to his chest, his anus curled towards the radiator's red glow in the darkened room.

Having told the story, Hector would shovel spoonsful of sugar into his mouth to stave off hunger, leaning over the arm of the easy chair to meet the spoon halfway, shedding grains on the carpet rather than on his trousers.

'What I can't understand about you, Hector, is why you can't eat lumps.'

'I'm not a bloody horse, man. Anyway, you never buy lumps.'

'I do. But you only go and throw them at me and then they get trampled into the carpet and crushed into the bed, and I have to sleep in the mess.'

'It's because we're so infantile, Freddie, that's what it is.'

Then, after another two spoonfuls or so, 'Why don't you go and make me some pancakes, Freddie, then I wouldn't be hungry? Give the stomach acid something to work on.'

So Freddie would toss pancakes in the kitchen, while Hector listened to the record player or read a book or entertained visitors.

Freddie's palindrome for Shrove Tuesday
panslopslipsluppulspilspolsnap.

The flat was low and deep and dark, reached by a narrow corridor, a steep alley by the side of an old house, whose ground floor the flat was. Little light entered in the daytime, for the living-room window looked out onto a bank of black earth, a cross section of the garden. Odd slanting rays of light might sometimes infiltrate from above, but rarely. And anyway it was at night that they were mainly there, curtains drawn against the earth, a small table-lamp with a red shade softening the room, warming the clammy walls.

'Dry up all that amniotic fluid, man.'

While the worms in the cross-sectioned earth waved towards the window's warmth.

Hector had a back bedroom and there was a kitchen where Freddie cooked, and a bathroom, and then this dark room which was Freddie's bedroom and the living room for both of them. At nights Freddie would curl up on the bed, pressing against the two sides of the wall, cramped into a corner clutching his legs, while Hector would sprawl out in the armchair, his legs stretching to the gas fire, telling Freddie stories.

'The trouble with you Freddie, see man, was that Puritan upbringing. Too much obsession with Sex, and not enough practice.'

Freddie pressed into the wall, and regretted soulfully his lack of practice, his inalienable, inevitable, imperishable inexperience.

'It's not your fault, Freddie,' Hector said magnanimously; 'it's just being English, see. Too much playing with yourself all the time. Makes you stunted, see; weakens your eyesight; makes you blush all the time.'

His sibilance was caressing, drawing out the blush along its length, hands fondling the rushing pumping blood beneath the skin. And Freddie would curl himself up closer and smaller and wipe his glasses misted from his flushed cheeks' heat.

'Now in Milford Haven, see, there was this mobile knocking shop:'

THE STORY OF THE KNOCKMOBILE

In Milford Haven there was a mobile knocking shop, that strolled the evening streets of the town. It would cruise slowly alongside the pavements of the darker roads, an old furniture van, driven by a thin, haggard consumptive, a damp cigarette always hanging from his mouth, the browned paper adhering to his lower lip even when he coughed, rackingly. Like all furniture vans it had a half door at the back that could be lowered to serve as a platform, on which to strap protruding pianos. And this platform served as a step, a doorway, a back porch. To which men in their needs would step from the evening pavements.

Inside this car of delights were two storeys, and a winding iron stair, finely wrought. And an old wooden settle from a demolished pub, on which to wait, and perhaps read the evening paper or a tattered *Illustrated London News*. And a garden of delights on each storey, lying in purple drapes beneath mirrored ceilings, lying there, waiting for you. Satisfied, men would return to the wooden settle and then, as their street corner or pub approached, stand on the outside platform from which they alighted at the appropriate place, returned to their chosen destinations. Often they would light a cigarette and stand in the twilight or beneath the moon, watching reflectively the van move slowly onwards in its regular course, rocking slightly on its springs, and at intervals the body tremulous with sudden urgent judderings, that never disturbed or impaired its onward progress.

During the air-raids of the war, it had served as an auxiliary ambulance in the daylight hours, and done sterling work, and it had been blessed by the Lord Bishop. It was painted a dull brown, like furniture.

It was a rack to Freddie, his penis's Procrustean bed. His responses could never be right; he would rise to the story, swelling with an enthusiasm that grew beyond the narrated details, baring the hopes he needed rashly before the circumciser's knife; or he would remain retracted, limp, huddled, flabbily sceptical, and would have to be pulled out from his Midland withdrawal to a firm understanding, to the erectness of man's reason distinguishing him from the beasts.

'Is that it, is it Freddie? Bestiality? Have you ever fucked a sheep, Freddie? Now up in North Wales, man, it's goats. They're slimmer than sheep, see, lither, more attractive like. Turkeys, too. There was a case at school once with a turkey; but I can't tell it you; it's too frightful, you'd be dreaming all night if I did.'

Freddie polished his glasses on the tail of his tie.

'Thirteen stitches I think it was. Just think of that.'

But every time he had polished them, he would fumble and touch a lens with his thumb or finger, smearing them again.

'You take your life in your hands every time,' said Hector. 'Take vaginal cramp, for instance. Have you ever thought of that, Freddie?'

'No,' said Freddie, in a voice that was a whisper; when he had sat listening for a long time, and then spoke, his voice would often be of uncertain volume. It worried him. He would sometimes make a trial utterance by clearing his throat, by coughing; but to clear his throat or cough made it clear he was preparing to speak, that he was unable to speak spontaneously. So really that was just as bad; and there was always the chance that, just speaking with no preparation, he would hit something like the right volume and pitch. He had tried to work out the statistics of it, but he wasn't sure what all the variables were.

'A friend of mine had to be cut out once. They were along the canal. Stuck. Couldn't do anything. Had to ask this passer-by to fetch an ambulance. Think of it, man. It could happen any time. To anyone. Suddenly, when you're least expecting it, when you're most vulnerable. People have died from it; it's like a tourniquet.'

Freddie clasped his hands and thrust them between his thighs, pressing them clasped into him and swaying slightly, as you do when, say, you have hit your thumb with a hammer, and press your thumb into you for comfort, to ease the pain.

Sometimes the dim evenings would be incandescent as Hector lit his farts. He would sit in the armchair holding a cigarette-lighter, his feet propped up on the mantelpiece.

'Wait for it, wait; wa-it, ready, watch Freddie, aaaarrrr-rrhhhhh, here she comes.'

And he would flick the lighter, holding it below his arse, to ignite the steady jet of gas.

WHOOOOOOOOOOOOOOOOOSSSSSSSSSSSHHHHH

'Isn't it beautiful, Freddie, like a neon rainbow?'

They were not short, yet somehow transitory. And so that Freddie would not doubt his eyes, Hector would wait, his feet up, his stomach muscles contracting to force out more gas, and light another, and another, and another.

WHOOSH WHOOSH WHOOOOOSSSSSSSSHHHHH

'You'll scorch yourself,' said Freddie, from the corner of his damp walls, his stack of books beside him.

'Never,' said Hector: 'come and look, see,' fingering the

trousers taut across his rectum. 'Come and look, feel if it's burnt.'

But Freddie stuck to his walls.

'Have a go, Freddie, here have a go,' and he threw the lighter across the room.

It was a long time before Freddie would have a go. Evening after evening he toyed with the lighter, fingering it, flicking it, lighting it, watching it burn before him; but to light it at his arse took evenings of familiarity, evenings of watching Hector illumined like some soaring skywriting flamethrowing falling angel.

And when Freddie did try his farts were little damp ones. Sssssssssssizzzzzzzzllllllllllle.

And did not ignite.

My farts are damp and do not ignite, masturbation is stunting, my eyes are weak, I fear sexual intercourse lest I am trapped by vaginal contractions, my society values virginity at the cost of health, organs not in constant use atrophy and drop away, one in six women in the streets is menstruating: our morning hymn is this, and song at evening.

Because Freddie was so uneasy, so uncertain of himself, Hector began to protect him. He protected him from incidents that he might not be able to cope with, from stories that might upset him. In the mornings he would get up first, take the newspaper from the letter-box, and then return to his bedroom and excise with razor-blade and nail-scissors incidents, reports, paragraphs, and occasionally individual words that he felt would upset Freddie if he were to see them, that would make him conscious of his own inadequacies, or of the corruption of the world about him.

'It's for your own good, Freddie,' he said, when Freddie having cooked the breakfast Hector got up again and let him see the paper, and Freddie looked at him sadly through the reticulations, a paragraph of obscenity replaced by a still, blue, sad eye.

71

'At least,' Freddie suggested, 'you could ink it out instead of cutting the paper to shreds. It's impossible to read now, it keeps ripping. I keep reading bits from the page beneath without realizing.'

'It only rips because of your anxiety, Freddie; your hands shake when you realize all the cruelties I've spared you from. Anyway, I can't ink them out, I keep the bits. I have a poste restante in Merthyr Tydfil and I collect them from it in the vacation. So don't go snooping around thinking you'll find the bits. I post them off as soon as I cut them out.'

And seeing Freddie's mouth pursed with annoyance in the large gap that had held a brassière advertisement, Hector poked a finger through one of the smaller orifices, and waggled it at him. Freddie made to bite it, but Hector withdrew in time.

'You can catch terrible sicknesses from fellatio, Freddie.'

At first Hector had been the sort of person who, on walks, peered through windows or climbed on garden walls. His curiosity had delayed him. But now he walked directly, with a straight back and an assured step; while Freddie scampered along beside, before, behind him, like a puppy off the lead, stopping at each tree, sniffing each lady's bicycle seat, gazing in every barber's shop to catch a glimpse of someone buying contraceptives. One evening they walked out visiting, snuffing the pollens falling from the roadside beeches, through the long uncertainty of the sun's late setting. Freddie, diverted by a chocolate machine or an enticing ground level letter-box through which to peer, or catching sight, maybe, of some acquaintance down a long street, delayed, and Hector strode ahead alone to make their call.

His feet were silent on the gravel as he walked to the back of the house to peer in at the uncurtained windows of the flat they were visiting, and to lie in wait for Freddie to give him a little frisson of terror beneath the high poplars. The garden was still, the grass soft and shaded, and bats flitted in the twilight between the poplars and the mock gothic turrets and gables.

Between the red curtains was a scene obliterating, momentarily, all thoughts of frightening Freddie.

The lights reveal a bed sitting-room with a central table, one armchair, and, conspicuously, a bed. On the table are three bottles of beer, one of which is empty. Two glasses, smeared with the vanished head of beer already drunk, stand beside them. A packet of contraceptives, torn open, lies on top of a stack of books. Beside the table, or possibly on it, is a portable record player, playing a Bach cantata. To it dance a naked girl and a young man, whom she is undressing as they dance, loosely, in time to the cantata, dropping his tie, his shirt, his vest, in little heaps around the room. Then she takes off his shoes, his socks, one at a time, slowly, gently stroking his feet, caressing his limbs as their nakedness is exposed; then his belt

Squat like a toad he watched, and then the crunch, crunch of feet on gravel. Hector sprang up, sprang and raced to meet Freddie in the drive.

'There's no one in, Freddie,' he said; 'let's go and have a drink.'

'What do you mean there's no one in? Have you knocked? He's always in.'

'But not tonight though; he's not in tonight though.'

'Are you sure? Maybe he didn't hear, I'll go round the back.'

'No, no, don't go round the back.'

'Why not?'

'Because he's not there, man; come on now, Freddie, come on and let's have a drink.'

'Well I'll just go and have a look.'

'No, Freddie,' he said, he shouted, he roared, 'no, you daft bastard, come on out of there,' and he grabbed his wrist and, twisting it up behind his back, steered him out of the driveway, scuffing up the gravel in the dusk and pushing him out beneath the safe beeches.

'What's the matter? Cut it out, Hector.'

'Shut up and I'll tell you when we have a drink.'

And until they reached a pub, Hector walked along silent, tight-lipped, like an officer told his supplies have been captured, and concealing the news till the last from his troops, not thinking what to say or do because there is nothing to say or do, but walking silent and alone. And Freddie trotted alongside, his mind fertile with invention.

'It's something too nasty to tell you,' Hector said in the pub, his upper lip moustached by the beer's head. 'It would only upset you; it would nauseate you, Freddie.'

'But what was it? Why can't you say?'

'It won't do you any good to know, Freddie. There's no point in having your face ground into the cesspit of corruption.'

'Maybe he was killing someone,' said Freddie to himself, to satisfy his urgent curiosity.

'Or being killed,' his other self replied.

'In a way,' said Hector.

'Was he being raped?' asked Freddie, polishing his glasses.

'Why do you think these things, Freddie? It can't do you any good, it can only make you unhappy to know.'

'Rape,' said Freddie to himself. 'Rape,' he replied. 'RAPE; rape; Rape; R a p e,' in different voices, different pitches.

'I can't tell you any more,' said Hector.

But it had been sufficient to arouse his curiosity and his flesh.

'Why does no one rape me?' he said; and he looked so sad that tears might have fallen into his glass and rippled slowly out to its perimeter.

A Note on a Lady in the United States of America

There was once a lady in the United States of America who, at the height and crest of her orgasm, called out, WHOOPEE, *in extasis supremis:* and achieved mention in a study of human sexuality published in the United States of America and later in Great Britain. Reviewers of the study remarked on her whoopee. And the couple who lived in the top storey flat two floors above Hector and Freddie appropriated the cry as symbol of their own own ecstasy and simultaneous climax.

*

'So I'm coming home this evening, see, quite late, see, in the twilight; and that bugger in the top flat is down the street in front of me. And when he gets near the front gate he stops, see, and he stands, and looks up at his window, and suddenly goes

WHOOOOOOOOOOOPPPPPPPPPPPPPPEEEEEEEEEEEEEEEE, right in the street there, like he's a wolf in the Arctic or something. And I think, oh God, oh God let's hope Freddie's not home to hear it, see, else it'll send him right off. And I'm thinking how bloody lucky it is he's not with me, when there's this other cry, out of the window, this female cry up at the top of the building, see:

WHOOOOOOOOOOOPPPPPPPPPPPPPPEEEEEEEEEEEEEEEE. And I'm thinking, oh my God, if he didn't hear the first he's probably gone and heard the second, and I'm thinking of something to explain to him about it so he doesn't realize, see, what's going on, when suddenly, Jesus Christ man, just as I'm walking through the gate and along the drive to the flat, Jesus there's suddenly another one:

WHOOOOOOOOOOOPPPPPPPPPPPPPPEEEEEEEEEEEEEEEE, right beside me like, scaring the living daylights out of me; and I look round and there he is, the little bugger, there's Freddie, perched on top of the bloody wall like an owl, gazing up at their window. And when he sees me, he just smiles down from the wall, like he wants to be patted, or stroked.'

'You try and protect him, see, but he sneaks through your guard, don't you, Freddie? The inexhaustible hunger of your mind scavenges for scraps to feast on. People get taken in, see, they get taken in by those round glasses and those innocent blue eyes, you know' – and he'd turn to the visitor and purse his lips – 'but it's misleading. He's got a mind like a rotting carcase, teaming with little white grubs, wriggling in their clammy holes, haven't you, Freddie?'

And Freddie would take off his glasses and rub them with a handkerchief; and because he couldn't see anybody without them on, he would be unaware of their presence, and sit silent in his little rubbing world.

*
75

He had betrayed his protection and could expect no more. One day he had washed a sweater and spread it out, on punctured sheets of newspaper, to dry on the floor, the way his mother had told him so that it would not stretch. When he came back that evening, he found Hector had nailed the extremities of the sleeves into the floor to crucify it.

'It's what the world does to the naïve, Freddie,' Hector told him. 'It's a warning, see.'

'Jesus wept,' wailed Freddie, tugging at the nails, which were driven in so deeply. 'How am I supposed to get them out?'

'You're not. It'll be cut down after death. I'll thrust a hole into the side with these scissors, see.'

'No you can't, it's my best sweater, it's ruined.'

'No, it's not ruined, Freddie, you can still wear it. Here, prise them out with a screwdriver.'

Gouging at the nails, and ripping the wool further, he prised them out. And Hector was right, he could still wear the sweater; which he did, proudly displaying the stigmata at his wrists.

It was the stigmata that first interested Marilyn. Freddie had worn his sweater to a party, and Hector had been relating some of Freddie's bizarrer doings, and Freddie had spread out his arms along the wall and tipped his head on one side and looked down on her, and smiled with a compassionate sympathy for his own failures, displaying the marks of his difference from mankind and their indifference.

'If you come round to the flat you can see the holes in the carpet,' he remarked.

'I'd love to come,' she said.

He hadn't expected that, and he looked across at Hector.

'Well go on, Freddie, what are you looking like that for, be a gentleman, ask her round to tea, don't dither, man.'

'You ought to have made a cake, you daft bugger,' Hector said the afternoon she was due. 'How can you ask someone to tea without making a cake?'

'There isn't time,' he said; 'and anyway, I don't know how to.

Why don't you make a cake?'

'You asked her to tea, Freddie, it's your responsibility.'

'But there isn't time and I don't know how to. I'll go and buy one.'

'Not on a Sunday, you won't.'

'Bugger,' he said; and then, 'I know,' he said, 'I'll make scones. I used to be good at scones.'

He was still in the kitchen making scones when she arrived, so Hector entertained her.

'So I'm coming home this evening, see, quite late see, in the twilight; and that bugger in the top flat is down the street in front of me. And when he gets near the front gate he stops, see, and he stands, and looks up at his window, and suddenly he goes – '

And suddenly there came from the kitchen –

'WHOOOOOOOOOOOOOOPPPPPPPPPPPPPPPEEEEEEEEEEEEE.'

'Oh my God,' said Hector, and rushed into the kitchen where Freddie stood with flour white hands, grinning, beaming through his spectacles.

'Why don't you make your bloody scones and mind your own business.

'It's as much my story as yours,' said Freddie.

'Don't talk bloody nonsense, man.'

'There wouldn't have been any story if it hadn't been for me.'

'Well I'm bloody telling it so keep out of it, see, you daft bugger.'

And as he went back to Marilyn in the living room, he could hear Freddie sibilantly whispering to himself, 'Whooppee, whooppee, whooppee, whooppee,' a whooppee to every scone he cut out of the pastry, a whooppee to every movement.

'He's got no shame, that's what the trouble is, no sense of shame,' Hector explained to Marilyn, 'especially when he gets nervous and excitable.'

'WhooPEE,' shrieked Freddie from the lavatory, flushing the bowl, his cry soaring above the crashing cascade of water.

*

When Freddie came into the room there was nowhere to sit, since Hector was in the chair and Marilyn on the bed. So he crouched on the floor, against his bookshelves, half beneath the table.

'No, sit here,' she said, patting the bed beside her.

'No, it's all right, I'm all right here.'

'Go on, Freddie, sit on the bed, she won't eat you, you'll be safe.'

'No, it's all right honestly, I prefer it here.'

'Oh don't be silly, Freddie; she'll think you're trying to look up her skirt.'

'I am,' and he crawled across the room, slowly, on all fours, grunting, his round blue eyes peering up. And quite instinctively she found herself tugging her skirt downwards and clamping her legs together.

'Oh my God,' said Hector, sucking sugar into his mouth.

But Freddie didn't prise her legs apart, and he did cooperate and sit on the bed, perched nervously at its edge, swivelling his head round from Marilyn to Hector and back again, and smiling at them.

Marilyn was lively, and dark haired and bright eyed and full figured and preoccupied with sex. She exuded sex. Her movements drew attention to her full bosom, to her thighs, to the lobes of her ears. When she moved around, and because she was lively she continually moved around, the bed tipped and lurched and dived and rose, and kept Freddie in a condition of unbalance, terrified lest staying himself he should rest a hand on her thigh or against her breast, drawn compulsively to resting his hands nearer those goals with every movement; except when he used them both to wipe his misted glasses; and, then, that done, he would beam through them at Hector in the chair, before swivelling his head back to Marilyn.

Hector told her the story of how they had met. Of how he would take off his shoes, his socks, one at a time, slowly, gently stroking his feet, caressing his limbs as their nakedness was exposed. And Freddie thrust out his feet before him and examined them through the rest of the story.

'Didn't Freud say feet were sexual images?' Freddie asked her.

'I don't know,' she said, 'but women tell the size of men's genitals by them.'

'Women tell the size of men's genitals by them?' Freddie repeated, reflectively, as if to catch the rhythm, as if not registering the meaning. Till he suddenly swung his legs down beneath the bed and looked at her, startled, 'Honestly?'

'Yes,' she said, as if surprised he should doubt.

'How? How do they do it? Do they measure them?'

'No, they just estimate from the size of the feet.'

'What, big feet have big – '

'That's right,' she said.

'Genitals,' he concluded, falteringly.

'Let's have a look at your feet, Freddie,' said Hector; 'where've you put them, have you tucked them away or something?' And he stretched out his legs to the fireplace, secure in the hugeness of his brown brogues.

'Why should I show you them?'

'Go on, let's have a look,' said Marilyn.

He shook his head, his feet tucked beneath the bed. And suddenly Hector leapt up and dived at him, grabbed his feet, held them both tightly with Freddie perched on the bed's edge, and pulled off his shoes and his socks, while Freddie struggled and shouted, helplessly.

'Aren't they lovely delicate little feet,' said Hector, holding them out to Marilyn; 'aren't they divine little feet?'

And Freddie squirmed and wriggled and curled his toes downwards as if to hide them beneath his soles.

'Don't do that Freddie; don't try and make them look smaller, for Chrissake man; stretch them out, slowly, that's it, s-t-r-e-t-c-h them.'

'But they're lovely feet,' said Marilyn, when Hector had let them loose and returned to his chair. 'They're beautifully soft. It's not just the size that matters,' she said, consolingly, intensely, 'it's shape and proportion and fineness.'

'Feel them,' said Hector, 'go on, stroke them, they're lovely.

Freddie won't mind, will you, Freddie? Just stroke them, they're like silk, like contraceptives.'

She stroked them.

And it was like nymphs' hands bathing him in nectar, nereids trailing their soft hair across his penis, mermaids drawing his throat between their breasts and curling their tails between his thighs.

'She's taken a fancy to you, Freddie; it's your small feet. She's got this big cunt, see, and wants to swallow you up, balls and all. Like the way she swallowed up your scones, Freddie; smeared with honey.'

Freddie sat on the bed, wondering.

'She's gone, Freddie; there's no point trying to rub yourself into the warm spots she's vacated.'

'I'm not; I'm just sitting down.'

'The way she stroked you, Freddie; so erotic.'

'It was all right,' he said.

'All right; ooh, you're a smooth man, Freddie; all right; I could see the little damp patch appearing on your trousers, the little spreading stickiness.'

He looked down at his trousers. 'It's not true,' he said.

'Look inside, man; put your hand in and feel.'

'It's not damp,' he said vehemently; 'and anyway she didn't "take a fancy" to me.'

'Why are you so sure, Freddie?'

'I just am,' he said.

But over dinner Freddie returned to the subject.

'Do you think she's a virgin?'

'Who?'

'Marilyn. Do you think she is?'

'Sometimes, Freddie, you really amaze me. What made you ask that?'

'How many men do you think she's had then?'

'Why didn't you ask her? Why ask me?'

'Two, do you think? Twelve? Twenty-five? Ninety?'

80

'Oh Freddie, for God's sake.'

'She might have been having her period.'

'Why didn't you go and sniff her bicycle seat then?'

'For periods?'

'For virgins too; acrid, a bottled up acrid smell, like airless caves.'

'I wonder if she's a virgin.'

'O leave it alone, Freddie. You'll never allow yourself to be guarded, will you? You won't be protected, you've got to be creeping along the ground lifting up the hems of women's dresses. You love nosing out the unpleasant, don't you, Freddie. You'll be trying to sleep with women next. Have you ever slept with women, Freddie? Have women ever asked you to sleep with them, Freddie?'

Freddie walked round the edges of the room, looking at the raised surfaces of the wallpaper, at spiders hiding in their cracks. But he was resistant: he would not sit on the bed and be vulnerable. 'Have you, then?' he asked, not answering. And Hector lay back in the armchair, his feet stretching out in front of him, and told the story of the woman in the Welsh hills.

You Gote-herd Gods, that love the grassie mountaines,
You nimphes that haunt the springs in pleasant vallies,
You satyrs joyd with free and quiet forrests,
Vouchsafe your silent ears to playning musique.

'I was hitching, see, in North Wales, one summer, hitching through the mountains.'

'When?' asked Freddie.

'Oh for God's sake, it doesn't matter when: just shut up and listen, I was hitching through the mountains, that summer, and this car pulled up with this lady driving it, see. Nicely spoken, southern English, you know. Not very old, you know, mid-thirties say. So she starts asking me questions the way people do when you're hitching, you know, where do you come from, what do you do, where are you going, all that sort of stuff. Then she says:

– You're not going to stay with your girlfriend?

– No, not at all.

– You've been staying with your girlfriend?

– No, I haven't actually.

– What, an attractive young man like you? I thought all students stayed with their girlfriends.

– Some do probably.

– But not you?

– Not me.

– And are you sexually emancipated?

'She didn't say that,' Freddie interjected.

'She did, man.'

'What, sexually emancipated?'

'Yes, she was southern English, like I told you; they all talk like that, try and make sex all technical, like something out of the colour supplements. All the English women are like that, Freddie; sex is like machines to them, cogwheels and meshes and things.

'And then she keeps on, see, how much sex students get, see, where they have it, how often they have it, who they have it with, see. So I started asking her things, about sex, you know. She was married, see, she told me that; got a husband.

– How often do you sleep with him, then? I said.

– Every night unless he's drunk, she said.

– So you get it seven times a week, I said, arithmetic see, Freddie.

'And she turns to me, just looks at me, with these still, brown eyes.

– Twenty-one, she says.

'Just think of it, Freddie, twenty-one times a week, one thousand and ninety-two times a year; you know what that means, Freddie, three times a night. Just think of it, just think of it, Freddie; three times every night, night after night.

– Doesn't he ever get tired? I said.

– Oh no, she says.

– Where is he now? I asked.

– Oh, she said, he's on business in Europe.

– So what do you do then? I asked. You don't get it twenty-one times a week when he's away.

'You know what she said? She said,

– More sometimes.

– What do you mean? I said. Naïve like. And she says, cool as a cucumber, her hair all in place, you know, just like you, Freddie, no shame, no sense of shame at all, she says,

– One has friends.

'One has friends,' said Freddie, quietly.

– Do you have lots of friends? I said.

– Sufficient, she says; one has to be discreet, a little.

– So how often do you get it when he's away, on average, say?

– It depends on one's friends, she says.

– On where they are, you mean?

– On where they are and on their performance.

'Think of it, Freddie, "their performance". It's like racing cars, or stallions: performance; all the time you're being rated on your performance. How often a night you can manage it; not just three times, but five times, seven times, more. And not just how many times, but how well – like racing cars setting up lap records, how quickly, how slowly, your tyres spinning round and round, the rubber burning on corners.

'It was hot, one of those hot days, Freddie, the sun beating through the windows, your clothes sticking to you, and in the car it was all clammy, all sticky. And I was going all hot and cold, see, every time she moved her hands on the wheel, in case she was going to put her hand on my thigh; but she never looked round, just kept looking at the road in front of her, never looked at me, like I wasn't there, just a voice, to ask questions, to speak to. Then she says, There's a reservoir near here, why don't we swim? and she takes the car up another road, off a crossroads, without waiting for an answer; and my tongue, see, my tongue is all cleft to my palate, and I'm too dry in my mouth to speak. And she stops the car by this reservoir, hills reaching up all around it, and a few bracken clumps, and these round smooth pebbles, these washed stones, reaching down into the water; and down beneath its surface the water is so clear and so still you can see them. And there's not a ripple on the water, just this still surface, reflecting the blue sky, and stretching out between these hills. So she goes off behind one of these clumps of bracken to change, see, and I just squat there, on these pebbles, playing ducks and drakes with them, just waiting, waiting and not knowing what's happening or what's going to happen, but knowing something will happen, that awful still waiting, all the stones clear and rounded sloping down beneath the water. And suddenly there's a splash and she's swimming, big powerful strokes, a crawl, you know, swimming straight out into this empty reservoir that's filled up this valley. And it's all so still.

'And then she starts to swim back, coming bigger, coming closer, till she's treading water.

– Why don't you come in? she says.

– I don't have any trunks, I said.

– Doesn't matter, she said.

'But I just sat there on the grass at the edge of the stones. So she swims closer in till she touches bottom. And then she starts walking up the slope, see, walking towards me. And I sat there, Freddie, like I was hypnotized by a snake, just sat there, this paralysing terror, as she walks up the slope, her neck and shoulders rising, coming out of the water, rising clear from the water, and then her breasts, her breasts and her nipples, floating on the water so when they're clear of the water they suddenly drop, suddenly sag, because they're no longer supported; and then her belly; and her pubic hair; her pubic hair, Freddie, water streaming out of it like out of matted weed pulled out of the water.

'And she comes up to me. It's lovely in, she says; why don't you swim, it's so beautiful? And she sits down beside me, water dripping off her, onto my arms, onto my trousers. And she puts an arm round me, a wet cold hand on my neck, and pulls me towards her, and I'm paralysed, Freddie, I'm just pulled towards her; and she puts out her other arm and runs her thumbnail up my flies, and then down, like she's unzipping me; but she isn't, not to begin with; she's playing all these tricks, all these games her lovers have taught her, see. And there's no one around for miles, just that reservoir, and the flat water, and the round smooth stones, and the sun; and the terror, Freddie, the awful terror.'

And then he stopped, the room darkened now, silent now his voice had stopped; and Freddie was sitting on the bed, pressed into the corner of the walls, rammed into them, just looking.
'So what happened?'
'It was horrible, man.'
Freddie pondered, waited. 'But did you,' he pressed, 'did you – ?'
'Oh don't go on, Freddie,' said Hector, 'don't go on, just leave it,' and his voice seemed to have a timbre of sincerity, of fear.
'What did she do then? Did she make you sleep with her?'
'Oh leave it, Freddie; I've told you to leave it; I've told you enough, now just shut up; mind your own business.'
'But – '
'But but but but but but – there's always some bloody but with you, Freddie; you're always bloody nosing too far; just leave it alone; stop trying to pry into things; it won't do you any good to know; it'll only make you unhappy; go and make some tea, I'm thirsty; you're just preoccupied with sex, that's your trouble. Try and control it, for God's sake, try not to make it so bloody obvious. What sort of impression do you think you make on people? What do you think that bloody girl thought of you? Just try and grow up for God's sake man, just leave it alone.'
And he went outside to make the tea and thought over what Hector had said as he waited for the kettle to boil, and that Hector should have admitted to terror, augmented and became his terror. And he felt not only that he was excluded from, but that he would never dare to be included in, the gaping chasms of the world of sex.

Hector now saw Freddie naked. He would come into the bath-room and clean his teeth at the wash basin when Freddie lay in the clear water of the bath, as naked as that evening of their first meeting. 'You should use sachets of foam, Freddie,' was his comment, 'then I couldn't see your nakedness.' And Freddie, without his glasses, could only blink towards where the voice came from. 'Let me cover it with spittle for you, man,' Hector offered; and his mouth full of saliva and toothpaste he turned from the basin, stooped his neck over the bath and blew out his cheeks, thrusting forward his lips, bringing his head closer.

And at times like this Freddie would cup his nakedness in his hands for protection and concealment; till his own touch excited him, and his nakedness would grow and swell and press against his guarding palms. And to reach for a flannel would be to remove a hand and let his shame spring forth redly and hotly above the clear water. All he could do was raise his knees, bend his legs, draw his knees toward him to clench his nakedness between his thighs, his hands cupped there thrusting his penis back against its pumped pressure (terrified of snapping it off like a green stalk; or as Queen Bees did to drones, as his divinity master had told them at school), pushing it for concealment between his raised thighs so that his body was like a woman's, which excited him still more. Till as he was pushing away, Hector would, peering toward the other end of the bath, as Freddie brought his knees up higher, his legs closer, say, looking at his buttocks now raised from the bath's floor, 'Lovely crop of arsehole hairs you've got there, Freddie. You ought to shave them, you know.'

He was standing disconsolately beside the Martyrs' Memorial one afternoon when Marilyn saw him. She rode her bicycle towards the kerb, and stopped to talk to him.

'Don't you think it's terribly phallic?' she said.

'I don't know; I hadn't thought.'

He was embarrassed at her speaking to him. He wanted to rush away into the familiar calm of the library. He had not expected to see her, he had never expected her to speak. He took off his glasses, his face hot, so he could see nothing anyway, however phallic.

'I wouldn't have noticed anyway, I'm depressed. Men get

depressed, it's their cycle, each four weeks; you know. If you'd spoken to me two weeks ago, I'd have been at the peak of my powers, alive, excitable, outward going. But not this week. It's not that there's any physical pain or anything; it's essentailly psychological. But it's got a physiological basis – hormones, you know.'

'Perhaps I ought to cheer you up,' she said.

'Oh no, that wouldn't do any good. It would be like, like – ' But he suddenly faltered, stopped.

'Like what?' she said.

'It doesn't matter; nothing. It wasn't anything.'

'Like making love to a woman who's got her period? Is that what you were going to say?'

He polished his spectacles, draping them in his hand-kerchief.

'Was that what you meant, what you were going to say?'

'Yes,' he said shortly.

'But you can.'

'I know I can; I just chose not to say it.'

'No, no,' she said; 'not say it, do it.' It was almost an imperative, in that great unsheltered intersection of streets. 'You can sleep with someone who's got her period.'

'I'm sure I couldn't,' he said quickly.

And he put on his glasses hastily and was about to rush off. But she saw them, his glasses, the one lens shattered, covered with Sellotape, the hinge bound with sticking plaster.

'What happened to them?'

'To what?'

'To your glasses.'

'My glasses?' he said. He laughed, nervously. 'Oh nothing. I just trod on them.'

'How did you do that? Don't you wear them all the time, I thought you had to?'

His eyes were weak, he had to wear them all the time.

'I just did,' he said. 'I took them off, so I wouldn't break them, so they wouldn't drop off.'

'So how did you break them, then?'

'I trod on them.'

'But how?'

'Well, I couldn't see where they were without them on, and I was dancing, and I trod on them. I didn't mean to,' he explained.

'What, you were dancing at a party?'

'No, I can't dance.'

'But you just said you were dancing.'

'But not at parties. I'd had a bath, you see, and Hector came in and told me to dance. It was in the flat, not at a party. And he was whipping me with his tie. So to stop my glasses getting broken I took them off and put them on the bed. But when he was whipping me the tie caught the glasses and knocked them on to the floor. And I accidently trod on them as I was dancing. It's all right, it didn't hurt; I mean, it could have done because I'd just had a bath and I hadn't got dressed. But I didn't fall on them or anything. I just trod on the edge of them. It didn't even hurt my feet, didn't even cut the skin,' he said, nervously smiling at her, in case she should be worried about his feet, after she had stroked them that time.

'But why did you do it?'

'Do what?'

'Dance,' she said.

'I don't know. Because Hector made me, I suppose. I don't mind really. It's the only time I do dance. I'm too shy at parties. I'm just not very good in social situations.'

But she cut short his inventory, his plea for stroking and sympathy. Her curiosity drove her.

'Was he naked?'

'Who, Hector? Oh no, he hadn't had a bath; anyway, he doesn't like being seen naked. In fact I don't think I ever have seen him naked.'

'Why not?'

'I don't know. I suppose I've just never been there when he's had a bath, or something. Or I've been in bed. I always go to bed first, you see. Anyway, he probably wouldn't like it. That puzzles me actually. I keep asking him why he won't let me see him naked, but he won't answer. At least, he does answer, but he never says. He just sort of avoids answering and says, "Never you mind," or "When you're a big boy, Freddie." '

'I don't understand,' she said, almost as if helplessly. 'How do you put up with it?'

'Put up with it?' he asked. 'I just do. I mean, it's not really a case of "putting up with", is it? But it's possible I won't. It's possible I'll change one day. I have been changing a lot, lately, you know.'

And he looked at her, so directly, so innocently, with his one eye, she felt so protective to him she wanted to grab him, smother him into her, swallow him.

And he drew away at that, leaving her on her bicycle seat in the mouth of a one-way street, so she could not turn round to follow him at once. And he was gone so quickly, hopping and jumping in hopscotch patterns and pirouettes that he invented – he was very lithe – that she could not call after him to come and have coffee.

> But
>> had
>> to
>
>> see
> him
>> whirl
>>> a-
>>> way.

One evening Freddie changed his mind about eating in college, and arrived back at five instead of later as he had said. He unlocked the door, wandered around the still kitchen, walked through to circumnavigate the living room his bedroom, sitting first here and then there, talking to himself softly, because he was alone.

The slight slap of water startled him. He cocked his head on one side, listened, and then whispered a soft 'whoopee' to himself.

'Whoopee,' he repeated louder, 'whoopwhoopwhoop-whoopee,' like the cuckoo in the middle of June: and approached the bathroom, calling as he went to Hector who was bathing there.

His fingers caressed the doorknob, caressed and closed and turned; his arm pushed the door open, slowly, gently.

'Bugger off,' shouted Hector, his voice reverberating in that undraped cell. But the arm had already moved to penetrate the doorway, the foot to cross that virgin threshold.

'I'm having a bath, for Godssake man, bugger off, you can't come in now.'

'Can't I?' said Freddie.

'No, you bloody well can't.'

'But I'm IN,' said Freddie, suddenly, thrusting the door through, breaking the invisible cord; and sprang into the room, his arms raised like a vampire's claws above his shoulders.

'Fuck off, fuck off, fuck off, you daft bugger,' said Hector; but protected himself amidst his anguish, grabbing at the towel on the hook behind the door, as the door swung towards the bath. And clutching it, he tore it down to him, pulled it down into the bath, its light green colour immediately deepening, and wrapped it around him, pulled it down against the force of the air it trapped, which escaped in gulping bubbles up to the water's surface. And while Freddie stood there and watched, Hector tucked the towel around his waist, raised his buttocks from the enamelled floor of the bath to wrap it beneath him, tucked the top together carefully.

'Just you wait, you daft bugger, just you wait till I've finished,' he said, to the smiling face, the blinking eyes, the beaming smile. 'Just you bloody wait.' And he rose from the bath with the green towel tight about him, and water streaming out of it like out of matted weed pulled out of a lake. At which Freddie ran, and Hector slammed the door shut, rattling the panes of frosted glass in the window, and locked it. Cursing Freddie for the ruin of the towel. And silence fell and the waters subsided.

*

When he was washed, Hector had to wrap the drenched towel around him to cover him while he went to his bedroom. He locked the bedroom door behind him, and dropped the sodden towel to the floor. He walked across to the built-in wardrobe, the evening sun tingeing his body a warm orange, and opened a door.

THE STORY OF A YEAR

So there I was, see, just had this bath, see, and I'm trying to find a bloody dry towel. So I open this door, open the wardrobe like, open the door and what do I see? There, all my shirts hanging on hangers, see, in a row, all hanging down, and then, in the middle of them, there's this year. Just among the shirts, a year, see, a yuman year, all still, not moving, not connected, just a disembodied year.

Oh God, and my heart starts pounding, see, pounding away, and nothing happens, and I'm nearly ready to vomit man, and I move one of the shirts, to see what happens, see if it'll drop down, see. And when I move the shirts, I see this daft bugger, his two round eyes just looking, and his mouth grinning, a mouth huge and unnatural stretching from year to year. Grinning.

It was horrible, man.

'God, you bugger, you daft bugger, damn you Freddie, I'll kill you man, I'll mash you, I'll chop you into little pieces.'

He stood paralysed, shouting imprecations, until Freddie moved from his waxen stillness. And then Hector recoiled, ran back, sprinted across the room and round the other side of the bed and pulled the bed cover, tugged at it until it suddenly loosened, its sudden release making him bound back into the wall; and free he drew it all towards him and wrapped it around his nakedness. Shouting the while.

'I'll kill you Freddie, I'll mash you, I'll burn your books, I'll rip up all your notes, I'll smash your glasses.'

All of which gave Freddie time to unlock the door and escape into the passage. 'Whooooppppeeeeee,' he called, his nose, glasses perched astride it, inching slowly, snake-like back round the door, pointing at Hector who was struggling in his improvised toga.

'You bloody ghoul, I'll pin you up on the wall, I'll stake you on the railings, I'll break your neck on the stairs, I'll drag you naked along the gravel. God, just you wait till I catch you, Freddie.'

And he ran, tripping in his toga, slipping on his wet feet, skidding on the sodden towel he had left in the door way. 'Freddie, Freddie.'

'Heckie, Heckie,' Freddie called from the living room his bedroom. 'Here I am, Heckie, Heckie, Heckieeeeeeeeeee.'

'I'll kill you, Freddie.'

'Hec, Hec, Hec. You'll have to catch me first, Hec, Hec, Heckie,' he called, leaping around the room, calling out in different voices, different pitches, different timbres, as if he were a puck. 'Hec, Hec, Heckie.'

Hector stood in the doorway, blocking it, his hands pressed against each jamb. 'What's so funny? F.L. Freddie Lawrence. French Letters. F.L.,' he called, hatefully, across the room, blocking Freddie's exit.

Freddie made a sudden feint, and as Hector moved to grab him the toga loosened, and his control was gone again. He grabbed at his falling bedspread, and lunged round after Freddie, who dryfooted and shod and unimpeded by that great drape, lightly escaped from the room and out of the flat.

'Whoopee,' he called from the gravel drive. 'Hec, Hec, Heckie; naked, naked, nakedy; nude, nude, nudie; Hec, Hec, Heckety.' And he squatted outside the window calling at Hector. And when Hector drew the curtains Freddie rushed round to the bedroom window and peered through that, haloed by the setting sun. When Hector looked up, Freddie realized, safe on the lawn, he had never seen him so angry. And frightened, he ran away.

He came back after the sun had set when the evening was grey and still. Outside the door of the flat were all his possessions, his books, his clothes, his notes, his soap, his pillow. Not thrown in fury, but piled in controlled anger, assembled, stacked, placed. He crouched on the gravel drive and looked at them, at the locked door, at the empty flat.

When he walked through it, the emptiness was frightening. He looked behind doors for hiding figures, but there was nothing behind any of the doors, beneath any of the beds, within any of the curtains. Hector's possessions remained; but did not fill the stillness. Not one damp footprint marked the floor, though globules of condensation had streamed silently down the bathroom wall. Through the door, which he had not closed after him, not one slightest stir of air came. And his own room was totally bare of all that belonged to him.

But it was not just the loss of his own possessions. It was a greater emptiness, a greater stillness than that. He sat on the floor unable to do anything; now there was no centre, nothing any longer held. He had seen Artemis bathing; he waited for hounds to devour him.

He was sitting in the middle of his empty floor when Marilyn bounded into the flat, nuzzled up to him affectionately.

'Are you moving or something?' she said.

He just shook his head, not even turning to look at her.

'Where's Hector?' she asked.

'I saw him naked,' Freddie said, his voice sepulchral in that bare room.

Her laughter trickled over the walls.

'Was it exciting?' she said, her tongue licking round her lips as she looked at him, smiling.

'I don't know,' he said; 'but it made him very angry. He's put all my things outside. I don't know what to do – '

'I came to invite you to a party.'

'I don't feel like a party after this,' he said.

'Oh come on,' she nipped at his heels; 'you'll enjoy it; it'll take your mind off things. You can't sit here all night.'

So he went to a party with her; and on his empty stomach she got him drunk; and pointed out to him that he could not return to the flat, since all his belongings had been put outside; and took him back with her; and gobbled him all up.

Freddie returned through the bright morning, after the rush hour, but while the milkmen were still whistling their way up sunny paths to smile at blushing housewives. When he arrived, his possessions, which he planned to spirit away, at least in part, were no longer outside the door. He stopped and looked at where they had lain, hearing the girl in the top flat singing as she made the joyous bed.

Oh don't deceive me, oh never leave me, how could you use a poor maiden so?

She opened a window to shake out a duster. Lest he should be observed he walked to the door, inserted the key into the lock, increased the pressure of his thumb and forefinger; but it would not turn. Only after he had fumbled for some seconds did he realize that the door was already unlocked.

Hector was in the kitchen. There was the smell of burnt egg, and he was wearing Freddie's apron. He stood at the table cutting bread, a new loaf which he was squashing flat from too much pressure as he held it. Their eyes met, and parted again.

And the apron round his thighs served only to remind Hector now, in its extra concealment, of his past nakedness, like those our first parents had sewn from fig-leaves.

While Freddie wondered if he smelt, if Hector could sniff out his secret. He wondered whether dogs could recognize the smell of bitches they had sniffed when they came to sniff other dogs, who had more than sniffed the bitches.

The table was between them, just lower than their loins which it served to underline, cradle or chopping block. Freddie's eyes sidled round the kitchen to see if his belongings were there. He wondered if to ask, and so reveal he had returned that evening, would be to open an entry for broader questionings.

Hector resumed his cutting. 'Do you want some bread?'

'No thanks.'

'Sure? Don't you want any breakfast? There aren't any eggs.'

'No, I've had – ' Freddie began, cutting himself short.

'Oh, you've had some,' said Hector, looking up.

'Where are my things?' Freddie asked quickly, fending him off.

'Your things?'

'My books and things.'

'In your room,' he said, as if surprised the questions should be asked. 'Why, did you want to take them away? Have you got somewhere else to go?'

'No.'

'Oh, I thought when you said that – '

'No,' Freddie chimed across him.

With bread knife and key they fenced.

'You've had some breakfast,' Hector resumed: it was the only entry he had made, the only leaf he had tugged off to clad his own nakedness and reveal Freddie's; he plucked at it again.

'So where were you last night?'

'I went to a party.'

'Oh; very nice too.' He could sense the uneasiness. While Freddie was so preoccupied in sniffing as surreptitiously, as silently, as secretly as he could for his own scents, his truffle's own hound, that he did not see the nakedness before him.

Hector untied the apron and folded it carefully, placing it on the table. But Freddie's eyes searched only for a mirror, in case this morning he looked different: curious, fearful, vain.

'A good party?'

'Yes.'

'Where did you sleep then?'

He had not expected Hector to be there. Or if he had thought he might have been, he had expected his possessions still to be outside where they had been the night before, so that he would not have needed to have gone in. He had not prepared an explanation. He had not expected to be in that kitchen again, and his possessions back in their place. And what explanation could he have prepared? Spent all night at the station? Went for a long walk and didn't sleep? Yet had they been there, his possessions, where would he have taken them? Where would

95

he have gone? Where was there ever else to go? And how would he have taken them, walking through the streets of the morning?

'Marilyn's,' he said; looking straight at Hector, but with his glasses off; and the blood rising in his face.

'Oh.'

But with his glasses off he could not see it when it rose in Hector's also.

'And did you sleep *with* Marilyn?'

'Yes, actually.'

'Oh. Very nice too.'

And after a silence:

'Was it nice?'

Freddie did not answer. He so slightly nodded or blinked, but it was not in response to any demand of Hector's. For Hector's question had had no force of demand behind it. He was demanding nothing; but asked questions, and elicited responses, from the formula of their previous life.

'Why didn't you bring her round to breakfast?'

'We've had breakfast.'

'Oh. Oh yes, of course.'

If Hector's hands missed a stroke in their sawing, the irregularly cut bread would not have shown it, so crumbled and gashed from his earlier efforts. And Freddie was looking anyway for a reflecting surface to test his appearance, not for signs of Hector's reaction, which he feared to know.

'You feel a man, now?' Hector asked, as a helpless gesture.

But Freddie did not reply.

They were both tired. Freddie wondered later whether Hector had sat up all night; but at the time he was more conscious of how his own face showed its lack of sleep.

It was a relief to both of them that so little, in all, was said.

And though the possessions were back in their place, there remained an emptiness, a stillness. At breakfast the papers separated them and there were no longer holes cut through which to exchange looks. Going to have a bath one evening,

Freddie had just turned on the taps when he heard Hector gathering up the books he was reading and withdrawing to his bedroom. So Freddie, having dried himself in the bathroom, was able to dry his hair before the fire in the living room alone.

He wouldn't let Marilyn come round. 'I don't think it would be a good idea,' he said.

'Why not?' she asked.

'I just don't think it would be a good idea.'

'Why? Is Hector disapproving? Is he moralistic?'

'No, but – '

'Doesn't he like me?'

'No, but – '

'Is he jealous?'

'I just don't think it would be a good idea,' he said.

So he visited her, and then usually in the afternoons. It was not possible to spend the night with her regularly since she lived in college. He had been terrified enough of detection just the one time. He could not accept her protestations that other people never worried. And to have stayed all night would have been to have insisted on Hector's attention; and he did not want unnecessarily to rub it in.

In the evenings, then, Freddie stayed in, from these various reasons. But Hector would be in less and less often, suddenly deciding he was going somewhere or visiting someone. And Freddie would be left alone in the still flat, unable to call on Marilyn because, since he did not see her in the evenings, she made other arrangements. He would sit in the darkening room with a book. He did not go out himself, from ignorance of where to go, and for fear, perhaps, of meeting Marilyn or Hector, which might have been construed as betrayal, or mistrust.

Freddie's feelings during this time were his own secret. He could communicate little with Hector. And there was no one else he could talk to. How could he talk to Marilyn about vaginal cramp and menstruation, premature ejaculation and simultaneous orgasm or its lack? His fears burgeoned in his isolation.

But Hector began to relax his withdrawal from Freddie. He still continued to go out in the evenings so that they were rarely together. But the papers, which he had ceased to collect from the letter-box and bowdlerize, he now sought again. And, with a thick black felt pen, outlined items for Freddie's attention. He would frame reports of a girl's nipples bitten off by a lover, of divorce on the grounds of buggery, of the side effects of the pill. Arrows would direct Freddie's wide eyes to women's page articles on premarital sex, the menopause, and primary schools with bins for sanitary towels. And when there were few items to frame, he would adorn photographs of models, adding thick black hair that curled out from beneath their brassières, and with a red pen pools of blood that dripped from between their legs. And draw syphilitic sores on the cock on the cornflakes packet.

'What are they?' Freddie asked one morning as he shook out flakes into his bowl of milk, pointing to Hector's drawings.

'They're syphilitic sores,' said Hector.

One evening Freddie was alone in the flat when Hector returned with a girl, whom he steered directly into his bedroom. Freddie glimpsed them as they passed his open door. Hector gave him a thumbs up sign and a grimace of a wink.

Freddie could hear them making love, the creaks of the bed, occasional words muttered low, and silences. Even if he stood by the window he could still hear the squeaking bed. And their moans. He tried to disregard the sounds but could not, and going to the kitchen for a glass of water he realized that the sounds came not only through the wall, but from Hector's half-open door.

They distressed him that perhaps he made noises like that, that perhaps Marilyn's low moans of delight sounded like that, that his movements were as noisy as those borne by the squeaking bed, and perhaps less rhythmic and regular. And running the tap to fill his glass with water made him want to pee as it always did, and peeing, hearing those grunts and groans while holding his penis, produced a tumescence he could not restrain, and that made him pee on the lavatory seat and then stop before he was finished. And he stood there holding his throbbing penis; but could not masturbate, now that he had a girl.

The next morning Freddie, who had slept fitfully, woke early and left without delaying to make even a cup of tea, but had breakfast in college. In the afternoon he visited Marilyn, but she had arranged to go out for the evening, so about seven thirty he had to return to the flat. For a while he had it to himself, before Hector returned, winking again as he steered his girl into the bedroom.

And then the grunts and groans.

He woke in the morning to find Hector standing beside his bed, wearing a dressing gown but no pyjamas, offering him a cup of tea.

'Here you are, Freddie,' he said.

The name was like a glove drawn back over him again, warming a cold hand, fitting each mound and declivity as if the flat were now swelling and contracting to mould itself warmly to him. He sat up in bed to take the cup.

'Why don't you ever bring Marilyn back, Freddie?' he asked, but not as a question, for he went straight back into the kitchen to take two more cups of tea and the paper into the bedroom. It was more a granting of permission or a request.

So the two girls met, Marilyn and Helen; over breakfast, which Freddie cooked while Hector talked to them at the table.

They became friends rapidly. The next two weeks saw them rapidly becoming, indeed, inseparable. And in the evenings they would sit together on the bed, talking, laughing, nudging each other to impress the points of their jokes or reminiscences, leaning back against the wall, or each other. While Hector reclined in his armchair, and Freddie squatted on the floor, against the bookcase, and partially beneath the extended leaf of the table. And one evening Hector began to tell the story of how he met Freddie, and it was like old times, warm and soft and protected, and Freddie moved for them, undulated round the room, and they were all content.

Become indeed inseparable, the girls would chat together happily in the evenings, on the bed, about clothes and clothes making, hip measurements and bust sizes, sanitary towels and periodic pains, brassières, douches, spermicidal foams and allergies to the pill. Sitting together on the bed, their voices, their laughter, their very bodies seemed to merge into one chuckling, throbbing, pulping eight-limbed presence, enmeshing Hector and Freddie with tentacular fallopian tubes, toying with the size of men's genitalia, the comparative duration of erections, the erogenous zones of the feet and ears.

They would cross their legs so that, for Hector and Freddie sitting before them, stretches of flabby thigh, tripe-like slabs of flesh, would be exposed. Hector would wriggle deeper into his chair, raise a leg across his knees to impede his line of vision; but for Freddie sitting on the floor, there was no protection possible for his upward gaze.

Held idly in the tentacles, Hector and Freddie would talk to each other, like missionaries in adjacent cooking pots, topi-d. Discussing the daily papers. And blocking out the shrieks and laughs and acres of stocking top flesh, it could have been like old times again. And at night just the gentle rocking of the beds, the soft lapping of the tides, the rise and fall of the slapping waves.

So that they thrived as a little community, swelling against the walls of that dark flat, thrusting the damp sides against the wormed earth. And the ecstatic calls of the top floor couple were blocked out by the happy clattering laughter of Helen and Marilyn, clucking round the kitchen and bedrooms like poultry oblivious of the whooping owl.

And with the warm summer they were all suddenly shot out through the narrow porchway to the hot sun, to the Italian villa that Helen and Marilyn had arranged, its whitened walls beaded with the sweat of their full bodies, its soft evenings drilled with the moan of blood-heavy mosquitoes. So that Hector's flesh rose in great weals, wide spreading blisters.

'It's all your blood there, see, all your poisons, raging in my skin. It's not the mosquitoes, see, it's where they've been, what they carry, who they've been biting before.'

With their bloods mixed so, with their shared sweats smearing all the clammy room, it was as if their bodies were merging into one single flesh.

'Sometimes, Freddie, sometimes I wonder who it is I'm fucking, see; whether it's Marilyn or Helen, see; I come in that thick dark sweatiness, man and how do you tell? It could be you, Freddie, some nights. How would we ever know?'

And at night Freddie would feel Marilyn's breasts, the pulpy line of her belly, with a cautious, guarded familiarity. Swirled around by the mosquitoes, the humidity, the intrusive laughter through thin walls, rattles and squeaks and sucking cloying noises that seemed sometimes to be his own, and sometimes not. And he would sweat further with a sort of fear, his stomach tensed, straining to listen, every dilated pore exuding stickily. Till Marilyn would whisper softly in his ear, 'Whoopee', and he would return to her, damply.

In the day they would walk through the small town where, to the tintinabulations of their delight, lounging men pinched the fleshy buttocks of Marilyn and Helen.

'Oh God, Freddie, I can't stand all these bloody wops.'

But Freddie quite liked them, and liked the wine and did not with Hector long for a decent beer. The girls spread themselves on the gritty sand, and Freddie tanned alongside them. But Hector, in long trousers and long sleeved shirt, crouched beneath a parasol, protecting his complexion from burn, blisters, skin cancer. Occasionally he would send Freddie off to purchase ice-creams; and when Freddie returned he would see Hector talking to the girls and the girls giggling. But when all four were together, Hector said little. And only when the girls went in for a swim together, would he talk to Freddie, unburden his complaints.

'We'd have done much better in Wales, man. Beautiful clear streams and cool mountains, man; bracken and grass instead of all this dirty sand.'

'Like that reservoir,' said Freddie.

Hector looked at him. 'Oh, that,' he said as if dismissively. And then, 'Why do you bring that up? Afraid that if we went, we'd meet her?'

'I'm not afraid,' said Freddie. 'Why should I be?' He didn't add the 'now', but that was what he meant.

'Are you sure?' asked Hector, discounting the unsaid.

'Yes.'

'Well, why don't we go then?'

'Because we're here.'

'We don't have to stay.'

'What do you mean?' asked Freddie. 'I like the sun, anyway.'

But Hector said no more, as the girls ran up from the sea, shaking water over them like affectionate spaniels.

And they lay still in the hot afternoon, the girls conducting a whispered conversation, lying on their bellies, the straps of their bikini tops untied, lying loose, trailing on the hot sand. But Hector would say no more, and Freddie lay there, his eyes drifting across to the girls, to the breasts. At which he would always feel Hector's silent smile, or hear the soft click of his tongue. But what else, on that beach, was there to do?

On the way back to the house they stopped at a bar and had a few drinks, Hector excepted, who sucked lemonade. And after the heat, the wine had an effect first giggly, then drowsy, on the girls. So that when the villa was finally reached, they withdrew to lie on the beds upstairs, leaving Hector and Freddie below. Freddie dozing after the wine, Hector reading a book and flicking his cigarette lighter on and off, irritatingly.

Yet their drowsiness did not drive them to sleep, Marilyn and Helen. Giggles trickled down the stairs into the room, movements, murmured voices. And when their laughter became strikingly louder, giggles descending the stairs with their footsteps, Freddie woke with a start. And turned to see them descend.

Naked they descended, naked they came lolloping down the stairs, their full breasts rising and falling at each step, at each giggle, at each hiccup, swinging and slapping with the movement of the descent and their giggles, and with their creasingsup with mirth as each touched and tickled the other. Into the room they came, touching each other's taut nipples, reaching hands down each other's buttocks to tickle anus and vagina, breasts and bellies swinging, hanging, sagging, pinafored only by their triangles of pubic hair.

'Oh no,' said Freddie.

And his heart was going like mad and 'yes,' they said, 'yes,' they said, 'yes.'

'You weren't really fond of her, Freddie, were you?' Hector said, as they carried their suitcases out of the villa. He spoke softly in case he should waken the girls from their drunken sleep, twined together on Freddie's bed.

'Well – '

'But you'll forget her, Freddie; she didn't mean that much to you, did she, she didn't care for you, Freddie, you didn't need her, did you? You'll be better off without her man, you'll see.'

'But – ' he began.

But Hector silenced him. 'Lolloping down the stairs,' he reminded him.

It gave Freddie an erection even to think of it, though one not only uncontrolled by but contrary to his feelings.

'It was horrible,' he said.

'There's no need to worry about them,' Hector assured him, as they walked towards the station. 'They're bound to have some travellers-cheques left. They don't need us, Freddie. They're all right. We'll be happier away from those two trollops, Freddie.'

At the beach Hector stopped and put his suitcase down. He took his wallet out of his pocket, and then handed Freddie a couple of cardboard packets.

'What are these?' Freddie asked.

'French letters, man; don't tell me you never used them. Oh my God, Freddie.'

'But she said there was no need, she was – '

'Well you can't do anything now, man. We'll see in the next month, we'll just have to wait.'

Freddie sat down on the sand, fear striking his stomach already so sick.

'It's too late now, man, anyway. It's all over man, it's finished. We'll just blow these up and then we'll go. So there's nothing left to remind us about it all.'

And he showed Freddie how to blow up the condoms like balloons, and knot the ends, and throw them into the sea. And the slight evening wind and the current took them away, like bloated jelly fish marauding the sleeping coast.

At which they continued to the station.

Her Most Bizarre Sexual Experience

I ask her, 'What was your most bizarre sexual experience?'

She is still very beautiful, that stillness, that glow. Her husband is in the kitchen with his girlfriend, taking some aspirin for a headache before he goes to bed. She has asked her husband and his girlfriend to stay there the night so she won't be left alone.

The question comes from the magazine I am looking at in which eight men and women describe their most bizarre sexual experience.

'Oh yes,' she remembers, 'I have had some bizarre sexual experiences. I was only young. I was still at school. Fifteen. And this woman. It was extraordinary, being all young and virginal. She used to invite me round to her house. And she was doing all these things. I only watched. It was only voyeurism.

'And the other one was this cocktail party. That was incredible, all these people in ties and holding drinks and carrying on pretending nothing was happening. And these two women in the corner. It was incredible. And people just talked. There was a lull at first. And then the talking started again and afterwards they just mixed in with the party and started carrying on ordinary cocktail party chatter. They just separated and mingled in with everyone else as if nothing had happened.

'You're looking very well,' she said, 'very together.'

See You Later

1

When he found himself in the valley it was already dusk; the night would descend heavily, suddenly, very soon. His glasses had broken and in the dusk he kept stumbling against things he could not see.

As soon as he saw the villagers, he stopped. He did not know who they were and was afraid of their possible hostility. In the silence now his stumbling had ceased he waited to hear them speak in case he knew the language. But now his stumbling had ceased, there was no sound at all. They seemed to move without sound, to perform their actions in total silence.

It was cold now the sun was almost set. The villagers began to move back to their settlement. He strained his ears to listen, but though he saw their lips move, he could hear nothing.

2

He lay some time in the short grass at the edge of the clearing the villagers had been cultivating. He tried to estimate how much time had passed. When he thought three or so hours had elapsed, then he stood and walked in the direction the villagers had taken. As he expected, he soon came on another clearing, scattered with adobe huts – single storeyed, rough finished, but quite extensive. He looked carefully. The one nearest showed no lights, had no sounds issuing from it. Its doorway was open. The odds were its inhabitants were somewhere in the centre of the village; he could risk going in for food, he had to eat; and if they were inside, the hut was nearest to the edge of the clearing and he could make his escape.

He approached it quietly, entered it carefully to brush against nothing; inside he stood stock still, straining his eyes in the dark to look round. A girl lay asleep on a mattress on the floor, covered by a blanket, except for a bare arm which she had reached from beneath it. She was beautiful, but it was not the time to admire beauty. He stood still not for the beauty of her fine-boned face, her rich black hair, but to make sure that he had not disturbed her. Yet her beauty entranced him all the same. And when she turned over, smiling in her sleep at some dream perhaps, he watched her because of her beauty.

And then she sat up. He should have left, not have stood watching her but left when he was able. She sat up, her eyes looked directly at him. He tensed himself for her scream. But she did not scream. Instead, she rose from her bed, the blanket falling away to disclose her nakedness, her full breasts, her slender waist, her slim legs. She rose and walked towards him. He had the insane fantasy that she was coming to welcome him to her bed, and he put his arm out to embrace her when she should reach him. But his arm, his hand, encountered nothing; and when she reached him, there was no contact from her rich warm nakedness, but an absurd ironic parody of love's hopeless ambition, the merging of two bodies into one. Except that this was no merging or interpenetration, merely that she occupied the same space as he did, for a brief moment, as she passed right through him, an insubstantial wraith. And it was he who screamed.

And he recoiled, backed into the wall of the hut, which instead of supporting him offered no resistance but let him pass right through its intangible substance into the village outside. In terror he ran from the ghost village and its ghostly inhabitants, pausing occasionally to listen for them following him after his scream. But they didn't follow.

3

He woke in the morning to the sound of crickets and birds, unseen, in the bushes and trees. He had slept at last from exhaustion; but he had slept uneasily. And he was bruised and gashed from running through the dark night.

He yawned, stretched his arms out before him: and they were

not there. The terror seized him again. He looked down at his feet, at his body: he was not there. Yet when he looked around, grassland was there, trees were there, a lake caught the sun's rays and glistened.

He ran, stumbling, to the lake's edge, plunged into it, felt the cool water round his invisible legs. He looked down for his reflection. But there was no reflection. Nor were there ripples when he moved.

He looked round and round: but left no shadow. Yet other objects existed; yet he existed. He could feel his hands, could clasp them; with invisible fingers he could pinch invisible flesh. He reached down to one of the round smooth stones on the lake's bed, to throw it and see if that would ripple the surface. But his hand clasped on something soft, sticky, repulsive. There were only stones to see, but his hand grasped no stones; just that stickiness from which he recoiled in horror. He looked automatically to see what he had touched, what stain it had left on his hand. But there was no hand to see.

Slowly he drew back from the lake, stood on dry land. He started to run along the stony shore. The stones gave way to huge slabs of rock, and he ran more easily than on the slipping stones that wrenched his ankles. Then suddenly he fell, plunged beneath the water, choking, struggling. He forced himself to the surface, struck out automatically with swimming motions, blinked the water from his eyes, snorted it from his nose. Yet he was not in water. He was waist deep in a slab of rock. Yet neck deep in water. His eyes saw the impalpable rock; his body felt the invisible water.

He swam an absurd breast stroke, to his eyes through air and rock, but his arms and legs carried him through the water until he grazed against some solid obstruction, and, scrambling with animal terror, his eyes useless, he regained firm ground. Visual reality became the tactile again: except for his body's invisibility. He lay on a rock slab feeling the sun drying him. He lay there trying to understand; and afraid to move.

4

Somehow, from shock, from exhaustion, he lost consciousness. When he woke he froze, seeing the villagers all around him, supporting between them huge nets, standing at the lake's edge. He feared they had detected him, come to capture him. Till he realized they ignored him, seemed unaware of his presence. No doubt he was invisible to them as he was to himself.

He watched one walk along the rock that had suddenly become water. He watched to see what would happen, like watching a man approach a banana skin. But nothing happened. The villager walked along the rock's surface, did not fall into the invisible water at all.

He was still fearful of arousing their attention, when one walked straight through him, like the girl the night before. Or not walked, but passed, glided like a wraith, a bodiless image. Walked through him not noticing him, and neither of them felt anything, and joined the others by the lake with their fishing nets. When they spoke together, no sounds issued; their lips alone showed that they spoke.

5

He had never believed in ghosts, but what were they if not ghosts: but could the land be ghostly too? Was that ghost rock, those huts ghost adobe? Rocks and villagers all looked so solid, so palpable: when they touched each other, their hands did not sink through their substance, as his hands sank through.

The girl came down again: he was enthralled by her beauty, that the night before he had seen her naked. Her beauty drew his terror away again for a while. He watched her for her beauty, not for understanding: but watching her increased his understanding, watching her he became aware of something about the villagers' behaviour. They moved their hands incessantly, as if warding off objects, or guarding against collision with objects, like blind people. When he watched them closely, he saw that they never stood and looked at anything; and when two did stand still, their gaze was directly at the blazing sun. It seemed not to affect them. He saw that they were not looking, but listened to someone calling from the distance, whose hands were cupped round his mouth: the sun did not hurt their eyes, they had no sight.

6

He was desperately hungry. But there was no food. The villagers had brought food, fruit and fish, and a sort of bread. He crept out to steal from it, crept though he knew they could not see him. But his hands closed on emptiness. Later he watched them eat it, eat with their so solid looking bodies that so solid looking food, to him so impalpable, commenting on its qualities with lively conversation, soundless to him.

7

He realized visual reality and tactile reality did not correspond. Or was it visual appearance and tactile appearance that did not correspond? Or was it visual reality and tactile appearance; or visual appearance and tactile reality? How could he tell; he was loth to surrender the primacy of the visual. But his body's hunger, his bruises, pressed on him the primacy of tactile realities: the visual did not hurt him. Yet why need that make the visual only appearance? Perhaps the unhurtful was the real, the ideal; like the girl.

Occasionally trees he saw would be there to the touch of his invisible hands. But their details would be different. It was this that brought understanding to him. He reached for the fruit of one tree. His hand clasped on soft, delicate, fragile substances that he would not see: substances that felt like flowers. He broke them away in his hand, felt them carefully. The fruit remained unplucked, impalpable. From the simple process of growth, of flowering and fruition, he realized what separated the realities, the appearances. Between the tactile and the visual was time.

His sudden illumination elated him. Having reached for fruit he had found flowers: a delay of, say, six months between the tactile and the visual: light waves delayed here in their travel. He deduced that to reach for flowers might bring him to fruit.

The pattern was not so simple: for some branches he saw were not there to the touch at all; and some, invisible, bruised him when he struck against them. But he found fruit: fruit unpredictably unripe, or rotten, as he reached his hands gingerly along the simulacra of branches. He eased his hunger a little.

But the light waves lagged more than a season. The slender trunk he saw had, to his hands, a huge girth. He could not reach around the massive unseen girth: yet he could have readily clasped his arms around the slender stem he saw: which when he tried the unseen girth prevented his reaching to, grazing his knuckles when he incautiously reached out. He brooded on the size. A tree with such a girth might be two hundred years old: the one he saw before him might be less than twenty.

He could never tell accurately. He took the figure two hundred for convenience, for an arbitrary certainty within the confusion. But it might have been three hundred; it might have been three thousand years. How long did it take the light of the most distant stars to reach the earth, the light of stars already exploded? Slowly, through the day of his illumination, realization spread. He might never escape the valley: if anyone came looking for him, on foot, by air, he would not see them, nor they him, unless they could see into the future and catch the slow travelling images of the present. He might hear searchers, for sound waves seemed as he had always known them; but he could not shout constantly to attract them who might never come: he could not light fires of sound like the castaway's smoke signal. He thought, momentarily, that perhaps he could: ignite the whole valley, and the sound of its blazing and crackling might be heard; but the flames would be sightless, so that he would never be able to avoid them, would be burnt unwittingly by invisible fire. And he could not find his way from the valley for he could never know its geography, its vegetation: he could use his eyes only with the sort of credence he could give to ancient charts and obsolete maps, without even knowing their possible antiquity. Earthquake, landslide, erosion, flooding, the shifting, changing, burgeoning of vegetation were not recorded for him, had all changed.

8

He grew weaker, unable to find sufficient fruit, unable to find other food. The villagers passed through and around him, and they grew familiar to him, in one way more familiar than they were to each other whom they never saw. But they spoke to each other and he never heard them. As he grew weaker, and perhaps delirious, he wondered if the girl, in whose room he sat each night, watching hopelessly over her nakedness which he tried and always failed to touch, perhaps had dreamed of him two hundred, two thousand years ago. He imagined that her smiles as she slept were smiles of her dreaming with longing of him, as he now longed for her. In desperation he would lie beside her, his invisibility beside her full visible nakedness, his tactile palpability beside her wraith-like emptiness. He spent each night beside her, watching her, calling her, weeping for her to respond, who had died two hundred, two thousand, years before. And how would she have imagined him in her dreams, she who had seen no man, not even the ghosts of her ancestors?

And sometimes he would wonder, half with terror, half with futile curiosity, who in two hundred, two thousand, years time ahead, might be there to watch his hopeless love for an object then no longer visible, his slow death creeping on him now, the final disintegration and decay invisible till then.

Aspects of the Dying Process

It was like any other party after any other evening at the pub and the sameness of it pressed on Graham, the secure comforts of regularity giving way beneath the nagging hope for change. But he remained. To leave would be to be alone; to remain would be to have the security of ever believing that excitement was about to arise, the conviction that things might happen he could not miss. And yet he felt menaced by it all, as if he had ventured into some enmeshing tropical jungle and was wrapped about by tendrils, lianas, pythons, and carnivorous flowers. Whose names he so well knew. All so hot, so steamy, so many limbs and such twilight confines. And he wanted to escape above it to the clear sky over the tops of the matted trees, where light airy creatures flew and perhaps gently perched. Though so hot and dry up there in the unimpeded rays of the sun, one could easily be burnt.

To see the girl was something of an answer to his hopes. She arrived with Fowler, and stood beside his interminable conversations about films. Well out of earshot, Graham could watch her undisturbed, her long blonde hair falling over her shoulders, over her white shirt, the whiteness, the clarity, the immediate attractiveness from his distance printing this sudden image on his ready imagination. And her bright blue eyes, her sweet naïve lips, her wide-eyed innocent eager expression, all so striking when she turned. But it was her slimness and her whiteness, that white blonde hair and the white shirt, that stood out.

When she detached herself from Fowler's group, wandered round looking at the room, he watched her, content for the moment to observe her light progress, her careful disdain of the environment. And as she passed him she looked at him with a quick acuteness, a sudden responsiveness of potential hostility.

'What's amusing you?' she asked.

'I was just watching you,' he said.

'Great,' she said. 'Am I so funny?'

'You seem delightful.'

She looked at him with that keen guardedness, reserved for unidentified spiders, or pools where crabs might lurk.

'That's more than I'd say for anybody else here,' she said.

'Thanks,' he smiled back.

And they seemed set to have an exchange of tired gestures.

'Who are all these people?' she asked. 'I'm sure I've never seen any of them. They're all so mangy. What part of North Vietnam do you think *that* crawled out of?'

She pointed to some pock-marked and emaciated figure. She spoke not loudly but piercingly. With 'mangy' her voice piped with a little girl's squeak, cutting through the dull hubbub of conversation.

'Why did you come then?' he asked her.

''Cause bloody Fowler wanted to.'

He wondered why she called him Fowler too, and not Francis which intimacy might have tolerated. Presumably to support the image, the filmmaker to be so well known that only his surname need be uttered. He did not ask. But she looked round her with unconcealed curiosity, stretching up, tipping up her chin as she tried to look over people (she wasn't tall) which showed the line of her throat and neck, the sweep of her long blonde hair setting it off.

'How do you get your jeans faded like that?' he asked her. Mottled dark and light blue so that they gave an appearance of fadedness, the current necessity, as well as, for the connoisseur, evidence of a complex and time-consuming process of artificial dyeing. She hadn't just sat beneath a gum tree and let the patches of sun and mottled shade settle beneath the leaves.

So she told him, in some detail, about the dyeing process. He heard her tones, her rhythms and pitch, though he did not retain their content. He watched the liveliness of her conversation, the enthusiasm in her eyes and cheeks and mouth. But he held off from touching her, exposed to Fowler there, uncertain what his response might be. So he just heard her. With a slight fear that the unguarded directness of her description of dyeing jeans might indicate not her naivety, but be there to expose his, so dumbly listening to keep her there.

'Do you want a drink?' he asked.

'Mmm,' she went, nodding her head.

'What do you want?'

'Beer,' she said, in a tone questioning why he should be questioning.

He raised his eyebrows defensively as he poured a glass: 'Most girls won't drink beer.' Who looked like her.

'I like the taste.'

'Most wouldn't think liking the taste sufficient reason for drinking it.' The dyeing of the jeans was not functional.

'That's a very bourgeois thing to say.'

'They're very bourgeois girls I know,' he said; to sustain the conversation and watch her eyes watch him, wonder at his seriousness; he hoped, at least, that she wondered, that she did not register as serious whatever he was saying, however he listened; the level gaze of her eyes was disconcerting.

He went out to the kitchen to get another bottle, and went on to piss. He wasn't sure how much of a little girl in white she was. Or whether she was barbed; so that when sobered he would notice small gashes covering him from his insensitive encounter. The innocence and youth that by her manner she blazoned might, its very emphaticness suggested, be merely the drape for some sharper understanding. And suspecting some such evaluating acuteness, he did not really expect her to be waiting for him to come back. He did not hurry. Yet she was still there, not moved from where they had been talking, and talking to no one else. She had her back to Fowler, who was haranguing a girl about some hypothetical film.

'What have you been doing?' she asked, impatient at his delay.

He poured her a beer, finding himself suddenly unable to say having a leak or any other of the ready synonyms before so cool, so clean, so delicate a creature. And seeing his silence, she suddenly giggled so that her hand shook and she spilled some of her beer which made her giggle the more. She had an acuteness of response to his silence that struck a strange counterpoint across her naivety of question and giggling. And laughing, she was pretty. She put her fingertips to her lips as if to conceal her patent giggles. She had all these mannerisms of a child, which he found touching, affecting.

And a child's impulsiveness. She reached to him and pulled from his pocket the folded copy of *Sire* Dexter had given him in the pub. He liked the simplicity of the way she did that, how she unaffectedly picked his pocket, begging no permission, the informality that seemed to imply an easy familiarity. But *Sire*. Its name, both hinting at *Esquire* to initiates hard of hearing, and yet evoking rather than the clubman passivity of 'esquire' the active pioneering life, the cattle station physicality of a stud farm; and carrying too the haunting overtones of a feudal *droit de seigneur*, a courtesying 'sire' of consent. And the nudes as nude as any, a little freckled, a little skin-cancered, but fleshly. He wished it had been almost anything else she had found in his pocket. Even *Leather World* might have suggested an exoticism of vice; not simple perviness. He waited for her to encounter the cover. That intimate gesture of taking the magazine could now result in the end of any thoughts of intimacy. He poured himself more beer. She turned the pages with the slow care of one not used to printed matter; she started from the front, turned them with the conscious motor activity of a child reared away from magazines or books. This way turning every page, absorbing each layout, each title, every mammary joke, all the grainy nudes. She gave the magazine an examination of the care and intensity usually reserved for rare items in museums and galleries, an examination conducted with a dutifulness rather than spontaneity, but a memorizing dutifulness to provide for the eventual report to be delivered.

It was impossible to tell what her response was. Any reaction took place without disturbing her precise surveyal: and since she was capable of showing reactions – he had encountered her giggles – it might have been that she registered nothing before those bared nipples and shrouded pudenda. He wished anyway he had left the copy in the car. It was not as if he had intended to look at it now. He was exposed by its nudities before this stranger. And even if she was unmoved, reacted in no way, then still there was a criticism of him: that in obtaining and carrying *Sire* he was clearly used to feeling some expected reaction. At which she might well turn away.

'Do you buy it all the time?' she asked.

'I didn't buy it, I got it for free.'

She didn't concern herself with how, but asked, 'Do men enjoy looking at this sort of thing?' As if she had been let out of her convent school for the first time that morning, and stood there, clad in her phenomenal innocence, amongst the crowd of groping hands and shared bottles, the aura of her whiteness creating a restraining, impregnable gulf between her and the crowded room. No one fondled her, passing to get another beer; no one stroked her buttocks or laid a hand on her shoulder, passing across the room. He could imagine Fowler, at first light of dawn on Bondi, crouching in the cold wet sand to film her against the inevitable sea, the bleached sand and the crested waves underlining her purity as she knelt there: and then no doubt lightly dancing back to the car she would leave Fowler to struggle with his tripod and the rest of the clutter, kept warm by the invincible flames of the ego of his own art.

But she had been let out that morning from no convent school but the bed of Fowler, emerged from no cloistral portal but the broken front gate of Fowler's rented terrace house. The innocence she had powdered on while the kettle boiled and whoever was the weaker willed that morning made tea. It was an innocence for aesthetic admiration but surely not of moral intimidation.

'I sometimes write for it,' he said, and then, while she still looked through, 'but I enjoy it, yes.'

'I can't imagine I'd enjoy looking at photographs of grotty men without any clothes on,' she said. 'I wonder how much they get.'

'Thinking of trying it?' he asked. 'Dexter was looking for someone.'

She smiled at him and tucked the rolled copy back in his pocket.

'What do you do?' she asked.

Which wasn't the sort of question asked. But he confessed to lecturing.

'I thought you said you wrote for that.'

'That's just – ' in my spare time, he would have said but changed to 'freelance'.

'Like a hobby?' she commented.

And had there been anything to reply he might have attempted it. But she continued: 'or perversion. The only lecturers I've ever met have been such awful bores, really incredible bores. Dirty unshaven men in raincoats with bad breath. They seemed to think if they bought you a crummy meal in a cheap restaurant they always claimed was a special undiscovered place only they knew, and I'm sure nobody else would ever want to admit to knowing it, and dredged half a bottle of warm white wine wrapped in newspaper from their raincoat pocket and then bored you about some ridiculous roman emperor or syphilitic poet you'd be dying to leap into bed with them as soon as ever you'd shouted them a taxi.'

'And did you?'

She directed her level gaze at him, not deigning a reply.

'I've got my own car anyway,' he said. 'I don't need to be shouted taxis.'

'Marvellous,' she said, widening her eyes and rolling them. 'I've never known anyone with a car.'

'You're getting snaky,' he said.

She put her hand on his arm. 'I'm not really being snaky. I think you're a marvellous lecturer and I'm sure your students simply adore you.'

He put his hand on her hand that was restraining his arm. So that he felt not the slightest aggression. And at his touch she looked at him steadily, with her impermeable impassivity.

'My glass is empty,' she said.

And going out to find another bottle in the kitchen, he was suddenly set upon by Marianne, who took him out into the back yard with her, and he could find no way to resist her demand he should talk to her. It must have been all of twenty minutes before he could ease himself away, evade her offer that they should go off for a fuck somewhere, and escape back to the house. He saw the girl standing by a group of people talking to Fowler. He had hardly expected her to wait alone.

'I'm sorry,' he said, and to his surprise she detached herself from the group to talk to him. They both walked away a space.

'They're all so boring,' she said, her voice shrill at the agonies of it.

'I'm sorry, I didn't mean to abandon you; I got caught up.'

'I saw,' she said. 'She's very pretty.'

'You reckon? She's a monster.'

'Monsters can be pretty,' she said.

'It's an interesting aesthetic possibility, but I'm not sure it's true.'

'I bet you didn't talk about boring old aesthetics to her,' she said, handling the word like an old dusty book she didn't want to soil her clothes.

He smiled hopefully at her, nailed now into a defeated stance of pedanticism. To engage her attention again and destroy that image he chose momentary honesty. 'She wanted me to fuck her,' he said.

'And did you?'

'Jeez no.'

'You were away long enough.'

'I was sitting on the back door step trying to argue my way out of it.'

'Whatever for?'

'I'd rather talk to you,' he said.

'That's very nice of you.'

He added, for honesty, 'She terrifies me, that rampant sexuality.'

'And I don't.'

He lit another cigarette. He did not feel up to holding the

conversation at the moment. She should have drunk more and been less chirpy.

'No, no, it's not that,' he said; and eventually, 'No, you remind of someone.'

'Yes, I'm sure,' she said, 'you tried to pick me up at a party once.'

'No,' he said shortly, dismissively, drunk enough to be brusque and uncertain of whether he might indeed have clumsily tried to pick her up. Clearly without success.

'It must be your sister then,' she said.

But he disregarded her, preoccupied with his search. Until, 'I know,' he said. 'Did you ever see *Bande à Parte*? Anna Karina, that's who you remind me of.'

'That's an awfully nice thing to say,' she said, her voice less warm than piping, but quite without joke or qualification; quite without surprise either; but with a contentment of acceptance.

'Is it?'

'It's the sort of thing any girl would be thrilled to have said about her.'

She made him feel very chivalrous, very elegantly polished in his compliments, like the hero of a romance. And cinécultured too, which we all have to be these days.

'It wasn't meant as a compliment,' he said, 'it was meant, you know, as an observation, as the truth, you know.'

'That's what makes it so nice,' she said. 'Even if her hair is the wrong colour.'

He didn't remember much after that high spot, nor how long he talked to her before Fowler came up and said they were going home. He remembered she objected, said she was enjoying it and why did he always have to spoil people's fun the few times she had any, and he said he had to be up early to shoot something or someone and she said there was nothing stopping him going to which he did not reply. Graham had the vague recollection later of attempting to reason with Fowler in support of the girl. And then they were gone.

Idle mornings Graham would walk through the Cross past the fruiterers and delicatessens and strip clubs while people shopped with a morning calm, late breakfasters strolling through the sun before they began, if they ever began, their day's later work. There was nothing frenetic; the morning papers lay unattended on their stands, the afternoon ones had not yet arrived for the sellers to shout their headlines, the strip clubs were open only for the cleaners, and poodles led on walks by girls in hair curlers draped with silk scarves. The few shirt-sleeved men drinking had the huge bars cool and spacious and empty. Having looked in the windows of the shirt shops and shoe shops and at the open stands of fruit, he liked to browse in a small bookshop stacked on every wall and mounded on its central tables with paperbacks, hardbacks, and little magazines. It was something he enjoyed to stop in there, talking to the owner about failing journals and flourishing books, exchanging fragments of news and gossip. It gave him the brief feeling of participation in the life and death of literature, consciously creating the illusion and happy to do so. He was surprised one morning to find Fowler's girl in there, crouched on the floor looking intently at a paperback she had prised from the bottom of a high stack.

'You,' he said feebly, surprised.

'Her name is Jacquie,' she said; and as he remained taken aback she added, 'you didn't know I could read, did you?' crouched there in white blouse and grey skirt like an eleven-year-old up to mischief, her hair falling over her face.

'I'm willing to believe anything,' he said, eager to believe she really was there.

'I can cook, too,' she said, and she held the book out for him to see; but she held it out straight before her so that from his upright position he could not read the title. He crouched down. *The Penguin Italian Cookbook*. He felt oddly embarrassed, as if he had caught her out in some misdemeanour, as if finding some-one in a chamber concert listening to a transistor relaying the trots. And immediately at that he felt caught out himself in an awful priggishness, holding his copy of *London Magazine* there as a sort of holier than thou thoughts of Chairman Mao before her unhallowed domestic practicality, even if it was a Penguin. And to be put in such a position of assertive superiority made him feel hopelessly conventional, hopelessly academic, before her spontaneity. Had he been carrying *The Penguin Book of Comics* he would have been all right. And so they both crouched there, behind the central pile of books, out of sight; and she began to smile at that, their crouching there, so close. But he was unable to reach out at her in the seriousness of that place, at her in that careful simplicity of dress.

And from their silence she stood up. 'I've found what I want at last after digging all over the place. Have you?'

'Have I what?' he asked, rising.

'Have you found what you want or are you still carrying on looking?'

'Oh, well yes, I suppose so,' he said. Which was probably a partial truth; but he did not feel willing to begin then to tell her that he enjoyed just looking over the covers and through the pages. Perhaps he underestimated her sympathies. But he feared her wide-eyed surprise, her laughing dismissal. And he was happy docilely to follow her, who did not even look behind, so sure of his following, out and along the sunlit pavement.

She talked, she chattered to him, about the warm morning, about fruits in the shops, about young men strolling with their afghan hounds, her hands gesturing, her hair swinging slightly as she moved her neck around looking at everything, her attention bouncing off the shifting objects of the morning. They had walked right down Macleay Street to the fountain when she said, 'Which way are you going?'

'I hadn't thought,' he said. 'I was just walking along with you.'

'That's nice of you. You do say some nice things, even if they do slip out accidentally.'

The fountain playing.

'I'm sorry, I just wasn't thinking,' he said, unthinking, automatic, her blonde hair in the bright sun his whole picture.

She laughed. 'You are a goose,' she said; but by gently resting her hand on his arm at the 'are' to underline it, she indicated an emphasis that was not to be interpreted as unkind. 'That's just what I mean,' she said. He was no longer sure what she'd meant, but her touch was a gesture towards that closeness he wanted with her. She seemed, in her lightness, chirrupiness, sunny happiness, her constant chatter and movement, a girl who would always be resting hands gently on whoever she was with, always arousing that tactile excitement, touching, stroking, enlivening. Yet she was not true to that impression. She was like a butterfly always hovering round flowers, twigs, branches, always exciting the stamens with a fluttering hope of contact, but rarely brushing against them.

'Do you want coffee somewhere?' he said, feeling now the aimlessness of his walk was indicated he must provide some other justification for his presence. But it was not the aimlessness of his walk: it was the exposure of its simple single aim.

She hovered, had only a short time, doubtfully: and then graciously settled on consent. They went to an outdoor café in the village centre, because the name appealed to his idle morning fantasies of a village. He wondered whether people who lived in the real village were conscious of its being the village and conscious of playing the appropriate or expected roles, derived from their literature.

'What village?' she asked.

He put his *London Magazine* and *Sydney Morning Herald* down carefully on the slatted table, carefully so as not to expose a backnumber of *Sire* enwrapped in the *Herald*. He did not constantly carry it, and did not want her to think he did.

They sat subjectless over their coffees, until she asked him to ask a passer-by what time it was, because she had to work. He'd never thought of her as working, indeed he could not imagine her as working. He asked her what she did and when she said she acted in television he was suddenly suffused with embarrassment at his all too clear remembrance of suggesting she should appear in one of Dexter's photo-stories in *Sire*. He hoped she would not remember, but something in his manner must have alerted her. Or perhaps she just remembered her last encounter with him fondly. For she pulled *Sire* out from its enfolding *Herald* and asked, 'Do you carry them round as a mascot?'

He felt himself beginning to blush. 'It's got a piece of mine in it,' he explained.

'Oh, I see, you carry your "pieces" around as mascots.'

'No, I just found it at someone's place so I took it.'

'To add to your multiple collection,' she suggested; and giggled. He didn't know whether at the image of his room surrounded with multiple mammaries or multiple copies of his stories, a monstrous grotto of id or ego. Or whether she was just laughing at seeing his name. She didn't stop to read his piece, though, but turned through the pages, nor did she ask to borrow the copy to read it. But nor, then, did he ask to see a videotape of her acting.

Those glancing contacts made him eager to encounter her further. When David Murray said he was holding a party and remarked Jacquie would be coming, Graham avoided the pub for the evening and went to the party at its appointed time. He was anxious to find her again, who was becoming his image of the unattainable, of whom he often found himself inquiring, talking. He found her beside a table of bread, biscuits, cheese, olives, which David's girls always provided. She listened to him as she ate, stopping chewing only for the briefest monosyllables, communicating mainly by nods, raised eyebrows, gestures of hands holding bread. 'I couldn't be bothered to cook tonight,' she said in one of the longer intervals as she cut and buttered a length of French roll and selected various cheeses and pickles to cram into it. 'And David always provides lots of food,' she added at the next break. 'If you arrive early. Fowler's moping like a starved bear, but I don't see why I should be expected to spend all my time cooking for him.'

'The Italian cookbook provided no stimulus,' he said.

'The what?'

He repeated it, substituting encouragement for stimulus.

She raised her eyebrows in continued puzzlement, raised her hands, bread in the right, a wedge of cheese in the left. He found her terribly attractive, like a poster for the Dairy Products Marketing board. And was filled with the same frustration that makes people rip off the poster across the area of the model's breasts, hoping for revealed nipples and finding only old posters; or that provokes the pencilling of nipples on to the taut, plumped out blouse, pudenda on to the jeans' crutch.

'The book I saw you buying,' he said.

'Oh that.' And some moments of mastication later, as she turned to the butter knife, 'You do remember the oddest things.'

And he was left wondering whether it was the book or the shop or the sunny morning she had forgotten. Which had lodged with him as one of his bright images of her. But she stood with him and when she had at last eaten enough, talked, and when they had talked, danced, the party by now filled up.

She was an odd, elusive girl. Dancing with her gave him a chance to touch her, briefly to hold her hand as they momentarily came together, his fingertips brushing her waist as they turned or passed each other; but these were only the briefest, slightest contacts. She smiled to herself at the sad music and smiling, danced to herself, pleased at his fluttering around her, encircling her, but not showing her pleasure other than in dancing there. It was not narcissistic, she was not dancing to admire her own movements; but abstracted. She did not resist Graham's stray contact, brushed hand. Nor did she reciprocate; between tracks she would rest a hand on his forearm in the silence. But there was never long between tracks, and she was quickly withdrawn behind the music's insulation. It was not a rejection, she was not driving him away. But a long suspension, a smiling balance he was to play along with. She allowed his contacts that she could preserve an enigmatic glaze.

And so it was until she said, 'It's too hot in here, let's move.' It was for him to suggest going outside. She looked at him, one eyebrow raised quizzically. He touched his hand against the small of her back, gently directing her through to the kitchen. 'I thought actresses weren't supposed to pull faces, to preserve their skin from wrinkles.'

'Most of the time it's not your skin you're trying to preserve,' she said.

He put his arm round her waist to draw her towards him, but

she slipped ahead. He noticed David grinning. 'You're wasting your time,' he said. 'You'll never learn, will you? You're wasting your time on her.'

Outside it was raining. They stood beside the door, sheltering beneath the veranda, watching it. He wanted to hold her thighs, reach his hands across her belly and down over her hips, up to press her breasts; he wanted to bite her ears so her neck would bend back, and her cheek rub slowly against his. But she remained quizzical, light. She mightn't want his hands pummelling her breasts, his teeth piercing her ears.

'Do you want to go to another party?' he asked her.

'Where?'

'Paddington.'

'At that same place again?'

He was touched that she remembered it, as perhaps she intended him to be.

'No, a few streets away.'

She nodded.

'What about Fowler?'

'What about your lady?'

They neither answered.

'Why don't we go then?'

They ran from the shelter of the veranda, Jacquie smiling as the rain swept across her face, spreading out her arms as if to imitate a seagull. They opened the back gate and he pointed out the car to her.

'I can't get in,' she wailed. 'Hurry up, I'm getting soaked,' and she clenched her hands together and held them in front of her, hunching her shoulders, jumping up and down on alternate feet making running motions as if movements for keeping warm would keep her dry. He tried the doors, searched through his pockets.

He ran back to get the keys, leaving her to huddle behind the car or fence. His thought as he ran back, was that her rain-soaked shirt would cling tight to her breasts, transparent. His thought. But she ran back in too to pick up an army bush shirt she'd left inside and draped that over her shoulders. As they were leaving again Fowler came into the kitchen.

'What are you doing?' he asked her, as she was half outside the door.

'Going to a party,' she said. 'See you later, won't be long.'

He could never remember whether he was driving her back afterwards to David's party or to her house, or what, Fowler likely to be home or shortly arriving, he hoped to gain by the latter alternative, had that been in mind. The intention depended on the previous scene at the second party, which was obliterated entirely from his recollection. He remembered on the way back aiming at cars coming from the opposite direction. He remembered being aware of being very drunk. On recollection he found it surprising that she had been neither censorious nor bored, which must have indicated that they had got on remarkably. Unless his lack of remembrance was selectively flattering. All was apparently fine, anyway, till he wrecked the car. They were looking for her house and she called out to him 'There it is', indicating a turning to where she lived; though whether it was the intention to take the turning or to drive on further to the first party and register this merely as an item of curious or useful information, he did not remember. He braked hard, anyway, quite unnecessarily, as a sort of joke, no doubt, either to stop suddenly or to pretend to stop suddenly. And they skidded sideways and downwards, the brakes quite locked, into a culvert at the footpath's edge. A signpost prevented the car from somersaulting. There was the crunch of impact, the sound of grating metal, the buckling of the chassis members, and the fan crumpling into the radiator.

He said 'Fuck', and switched off the ignition. She joined him on the footpath, and they looked at the caved-in grille, the crumpled wing, the nearside front wheel forced into an irretrievable position.

'Oh, you silly goose,' she said.

And on his refusing coffee, and the necessary abandonment of the car, ran lightly through the drizzle home to Fowler.

*

He saw her unexpectedly the next week. There was a reception for a distinguished writer. Graham took Judy along, making amends, marking a new order of life. Not that they either especially wanted to receive the distinguished writer; but it was the gesture of an activity together.

And then, standing at the bar, he heard the familiar piping voice.

'Hello professor,' she called.

He turned round and saw her standing there, radiant, smiling, Fowler trapped by two blue-rinsed sexagenarian cinéasts some way behind.

He smiled at her and asked if she wanted a drink.

'I shouldn't think you do, professor,' she said.

'I'm all right.'

'How's your car, professor?'

'Look, I don't have a chair.'

'Or a car, Dr Coburn.'

'I don't have a doctorate.'

'Lecturer Coburn.'

'Why are you so happy, anyway?' he asked.

'At seeing you, Lecturer Coburn.' And he might have believed her, but could not afford to.

'Why are you so gloomy, then?' she asked.

And where could he begin? 'The car's a write-off,' he said.

'I thought that might happen,' she said.

'What do you mean, you thought that *might* happen, you were in it.'

'Driving back from that party I thought it might happen,' she said.

'Great. Why didn't you say?'

'I did but you wouldn't listen.'

'Oh hell,' he said, for it was all too probable. And if she were lying, that was all too probable too.

'And what did your lady say?' she asked.

'When?'

'About the car.'

'I've forgotten,' he said. 'I can't bear to remember, it's too painful.'

'I thought it might be,' she said.

He was about to ask what Fowler had said, but she cut across him, 'Do you think I ought to seduce this writer man? Do you think it might cause an international incident?'

'It could, no doubt.'

'How marvellous,' she said.

Even if her elation was due to nothing of his, it was still delightful to be showered by it. And he was showered by it. She treated him with the enthusiastic curiosity of a child taken to the zoo, touching his arm to attract his attention, using his shoulder to raise herself to look above the crowd. His avuncular role had its compensations. Yet he wondered at her capacity for self-deceit or for selective memory; he wondered how she could have been unaware of his motives, his aspirations, at that party; how could she treat him with her child's condescension now unless she were unbelievably unaware? Or was all that a façade she used to deceive Fowler; or perhaps to discourage the unwelcome or intrusive, in whose number she perhaps placed him. Though wouldn't a frigid distance, a rude disdain, have been a surer barrier? And so she swung round him, a brighter moth for his candle than the camphored poetesses, at least.

Judy came across because he had the cigarettes; and though he introduced them to each other, the chill was unbreakable. Afterwards he was furious within himself with Judy, though shamed enough by his car-wrecking, and its events, not to express this: but the fault was not only Judy's. Jacquie's brightness was suddenly withdrawn, and she ceased to respond or react; her hostility was directed not so much at Judy, for whom, certainly, she showed no enthusiasm, but at Graham, at Graham for still being with her, for taking her to this reception, for introducing her. For it demonstrated that though she had achieved the ready destruction of his car at that party, she had effected no thorough break from his lady. She said, 'Thank you for the drink,' and turned away, turned around until she saw Fowler, and then walked directly towards him.

'Sorry,' said Judy, 'I didn't mean to intrude.'

Which left him no easy outlet for his aggressions, for he could hardly blame her for Jacquie's chosen manner.

And he would have ignored Jacquie from then onwards, had he not seen her later standing alone, not in any sought isolation for elegant display, but in utter loss. People were in clusters around the distinguished writer, around the bar, around other satellite centres. But she stood in one corner of the room, away from everyone. And he joined her again, not wanting her terse withdrawal to be their final encounter, and suspecting that she felt alone, knowing no one.

'Are you still going to seduce him?'

She turned listlessly: 'Who?'

'The distinguished guest.'

'I never seduce people,' she said, her black dress enfolding and dwarfing her, her blonde hair and white make-up giving her a chill pallor, a blankness.

'You let them seduce you,' he said, cheerily; for everyone else was cheery.

'No.'

And he felt himself blushing, his exuded warmth bouncing back from the impermeable glass of her chillness and charging his own cheeks. He opened his mouth to speak but found he was without anything to say. He looked down at his drink; if he drained it quickly he could politely escape on the excuse of going to the bar. Though she scarcely encouraged politeness, who, having turned from him in contempt, now froze him away.

But as suddenly she changed; not relented, though he could have interpreted it as that; and, her lashes fluttering over tears that had they not been despite their salinity frozen must have slipped out, asked in her most importuning, dependent voice, would he get her a drink, please. And almost tempted to refuse, he was moved by the please; though still not certain that on returning from the bar he would find her there. But she stayed. While at the bar Fowler talked to some elegant socialite blonde for whom he was buying drinks.

Jacquie moved her mouth into a smile, as for a camera, at his bringing her a drink. 'I've got no money,' she said. And he understood that Fowler had abandoned her for the moment, no doubt in response to her last week's abandonment of him. Graham wondered about fostering her, spiriting her away, but he had no car in which to take her, and had Judy with him anyway. He did not, though, reject the idea, but let it lie there; he would not deflect their conversation from reaching towards that.

But there was no conversation to deflect. Without her enthusiasm she was nothing. Without her vivacity, she was in suspension. She had not read anything by the distinguished writer nor was she interested in discussing him; she seemed not to have read anything; she could remember no films she had seen; and films served only to nail down the image of Fowler into her consciousness, with the girl by the bar. She offered nothing, nor would she respond to Graham's offerings. She existed there like a human form preserved on ice, ready for an alien consciousness to assume her shape and suspended personality. And come, it was to be hoped, with a richer information stock than she was equipped with. Entered by this cosmic traveller, triggered off by its energies, her heart and pulse rate stepped up from their hibernatory minimum, she would swirl through the crowded room with the suddenly unrestrained momentum of a dervish. But now she existed in suspension. And finally tired, even, of standing she moved to a couch at the corner of the room from where she could watch, with total preoccupation, with the concentration indeed of a planetary alien observing social behaviour for later assumption, Fowler's charm. Graham stood beside her, not even participant in her silence for it was a totally private thing. If like Alice she could have wept, she would have drowned the whole assembly without forethought or compunction, perhaps, indeed, without awareness.

He left her. She put out no hands to hold him, reached out for no support. She curled into herself, and made no appeal. No voiced appeal; perhaps her manner now was the fullest appeal, the only real appeal she could ever make. For she was utterly without protection. But in putting no protection between her and the world, putting no guise of capability that would invite support, she failed also to put anything at all. The world ceased to exist for her, its bonds, its offers, were excluded. Graham did not resist. He accepted his exclusion. His predominant feeling, indeed, had no relationship to her, who now insulated herself from relationships. His annoyance was directed at himself, for having wasted time on her, for having imaged her so often, for having deluded himself with hopeless fantasies; not least for the wreck of his car. He saw for the first time that blank emptiness, that beautifully shaped hollowness, that David, that Marianne, that everyone had told him of, he saw for the first time what they had always seen; and the feeling that predominated for him now was related to the appearance of stupidity he must have presented to everyone else in his pursuit of her, rather than to the engulfing stupidity and petty emptiness she now presented to him. And perhaps her all-consuming selfishness had spread to him; yet how could he be outgoing to her who refused all gestures? He left her there. Slumped on the couch, she no longer seemed even attractive.

Although the reception had been organized by the Brotherhood of Australian Writers, it was the distinguished guest's prime interest, as the evening developed and he was bought more drinks, to encounter neither brothers nor writers, but as many of the antipodean sisterhood as his literate hands, his typewriter calloused fingertips, could grasp. Some of the shoulders and backs and waists, some of the bosoms glancingly brushed, might conceivably have belonged to writers; indeed he had initially to fondle the aged literary ladies, he had to be kissed by their powdered lips and nuzzled by their affectionate wrinkled cheeks and pierced by their hysteric giggles. But by judicious movements and intersections, he encountered the prettiest of the younger offerings and Fowler intelligently re-encountered Jacquie and bore her to the distinguished guest's hecatomb. Who was charmed and seized; they made intense trysts beneath Fowler's benign gaze. As Graham left at the evening's end, Fowler and Jacquie were planning the evening's itinerary for the great novelist, planning his intimate tour of the town. They did not notice Graham's departure.

He withdrew into himself the entire taxi ride home, an introspective revaluation that to Judy appeared merely as a sulk. He considered the brief hint of a consolation in a story for his great-nieces, of how he smashed up his car with a girl three nights later seduced by an internationally celebrated novelist. But how could he explain to his grandchildren that after so intimate a carsmashing he should be so instantly excluded? He toyed with the images of Fowler's ogredom, pimping Jacquie for the rights to a film of one of the writer's trilogies. He wondered what had happened to the blonde at the bar, so readily dispensable. And had he, too, been as readily dispensable a part in some other game they had been playing; who, when it came to the prime values of their careers responded with a glorious unanimity of purpose, of plan? He was miserable with drinking, with loss, with the waste of an evening in which he had not even said a word to the celebrity, not even acquired a photograph for posterity.

One soporific and humid afternoon his tutorial was awoken by the ringing of his phone.

'There's somebody wants to see you,' said the department secretary.

'I've got a class.'

'It seems to be important.'

'Oh Christ,' he said and was not happy. 'Who is it?'

'A Miss Fowler.'

'Who's that?'

'I don't know, it's you she knows.'

'Well, tell her to come over at the end of the hour.'

There was silence as a hand over the mouthpiece muffled the relayed message and reply.

'She hasn't got the time.'

'Oh hell, well send her over now. Can't she speak to me on the phone?' He couldn't think what it could be, who she was; he felt slightly sick with unhappy expectation.

'No, she wants to see you personally; and she doesn't understand the directions to get to your room.'

'I'll come over,' he said, and shuffled around his desk for cigarettes. He apologized to his class and asked them to wait.

'Christ, it's you,' he said when he saw Jacquie. With relief that out of all the possibilities, it was not one of the unmentionable, unthinkable ones.

'You are difficult to get on to,' she said.

'It's my only defence.'

She pulled a face. She'd been standing by the window, diverting herself by looking out of it until he came. The sun glinted on her blonde hair.

'Well, what can I do for you?' he asked. He stood by the door, holding it open, indicating by that that she was to follow him out. The secretary was inhibiting.

'Where are you going?'

'Well, we can't stand here all day.'

'It's a very nice room,' she said.

'Sure, but it's not mine. Come on to the – ' He wanted the sentence to tail away as they left the office.

'To the where?' she asked, slowly withdrawing from the patch of sun by the window.

'To the staff room.'

'I'd love a drink.'

He attempted a look of much put on innocence, of exhausted resignation, as he shut the door, by way of exoneration before the secretary. But Jacquie opened the door again immediately and looked back in: 'Thank you ever so much,' she said in her sweetest voice.

He suppressed his welling sighs. 'Look, I'm teaching,' he said. 'Are you in a hurry or could – '

'I'm just dying for a drink.'

'So am I but I can't have one for another forty minutes.'

'Say you're sick, say you can't get there.'

'They know I can get there, I've been there already.'

'Well, say you had an urgent phone call.'

She was so bright, so lively, so happy, all that first attraction for her flooded back.

'I did – look, what is all the urgency?'

'Nothing,' she said, 'I just felt I'd like to see you.'

'That's very nice of you, but – '

'Oh, if it's going to be all buts I'll go, sorry to be a nuisance.'

She held out her hand for him to shake goodbye. He took it, for any touch of her. She let it rest in his, lightly, even limply; and watched him with that level gaze.

'Let's go to the common room.'

'Can I get a drink there?'

'Coffee.'

'I don't want coffee.'

'Hell – '

'Why don't we have a beer?'

'I've got to teach,' he wailed.

'Phone them up and say you've been suddenly overcome by something.'

'I suppose I have,' he said: she was a good enough actress to know how to feed lines. 'We still have to go to the staff room to phone.'

'What's wrong with the secretary's phone?' she asked.

'Why did you call yourself Miss Fowler?' he asked, walking to the bar.

'I said Mrs, actually.'

He looked in sudden alarm at her hand, but there was no ring. She laughed.

'I didn't think you'd know my name so I thought that if I used Fowler's you'd know who I was.'

'Oh,' he said, and then, recognizing that it wouldn't have been just to have a drink with him that she would have come, asked, 'What are you doing here anyway?' Any hope that she might have left Fowler and wanted his support vanished. Else how could she have used Fowler's name?

'You'd never guess,' she said. 'I was judging a beauty competition.'

He could have guessed, because Dexter had told him about it

and was planning to come up to persuade the winner to pose for *Sire*. But he said nothing.

'We're closed,' the lady at the bar said.

'Can't we get a drink at all?'

'Not even just a small one?' Jacquie pleaded, her head on one side, her slim grey dress with its white collar and cuffs making her look both childlike innocent and under age.

'You'll have to buy bottles.'

'You mean we have to drink out of the bottle?' Jacquie asked, wide-eyed. 'Have you got any straws?'

The lady at the bar scrutinized her, but detected no malice.

'We'll have a bottle then,' Graham said.

'Will one be enough? I'm not opening up again.'

'You're thirsty?' he asked Jacquie. She nodded vigorously, eyes wide for a treat, so he bought three.

She lay back in a low chair, letting her arms drop limp over the chair's sides, letting her feet slide out along the floor, her legs long, slender. The sun poured over her through the window.

'You can't imagine anything worse than judging a stupid beauty competition on a day like this.'

'I can imagine a lot of things worse.'

'The trouble with you, Dr Coburn, is you're just a dirty old perv.'

'I'm not a doctor,' he said.

'And you're not old, not that old, really.'

'Great.'

'It must be perving at all those students all day makes you look old, gives you lines round your eyes or something.'

'Why didn't you invite me to the beauty contest, it sounds just right for me?'

'Ugh,' she said, 'all those bodies. The smell was foul, sweaty, flabby bodies in swimsuits. You'd think they'd never heard of deodorants. It was dreadful. All those daggy girls. And hundreds of alfish men groping around – it was like Noah's ark, really it was, all those alfs belching beer all over you and wanting to paw you with their sweaty hands. Ugh.' And she really did shudder.

'Probably engineering students,' he said, automatically.

'I wouldn't have been surprised if they'd been lecturers.'

He wanted to reach out and touch her and draw her towards him, but she preserved this cool distance as much as ever. At first he had been intrigued by her carrying that aura of innocence and childlikeness in a life that took her through the pub, her acting world, to cohabiting presence of Fowler. He'd found the combination poignantly appealing: but he'd never doubted that the innocence wasn't anything other than a style, he'd never doubted that, since she was living with Fowler she would naturally go to bed with someone who attracted her. He had never assumed her style was anything other than an appealing manner. He wondered now, though, whether he had been totally misled, wondered whether she didn't hold that manner with the ferocity of a moral commitment. And yet the episode of the distinguished writer had to be reconciled with this; and yet with this, this image of innocence, could there have been an episode after all? Perhaps the writer, too, had simply wrecked a car for her and gone his way.

He was beginning with the beer to feel a little sleepy. A small guilt prodded him about his tutorial beneath his calm; but he was committed to a lifestyle of spontaneity; he resisted the grey-suited norm of the bar at lunchtime; and there was no one at all but the two of them in the bar through the afternoon. It was an enclave of peace amidst the heat and activity.

'I hope you don't get the sack because of me,' she said, and stopped herself from laughing, biting her lip in a way that drew attention to the suppressed laughter.

'Bloody liar,' he said. 'You know you'd just love me to get the sack because of you.'

She looked at him impassively.

'Such devotion,' he glossed.

Liveliness spread over her face. 'It would be rather marvellous, wouldn't it?' she said. 'It's the sort of thing any girl would be thrilled to have done for her.'

'And you think I'm crazy enough to do it?'

'Not deliberately,' she said.

He moved to pour her another drink, but she put her hand over the glass.

'You've hardly had any.'

'I have,' she said. 'I don't want any more, I'm not thirsty now.'

He held the bottle and looked at the two full ones on the table. The tops had already been removed so they could not be returned.

'You'll be able to drink them,' she said.

After they had sat warm and peaceful in the sun, and time had passed, and by talking they had established an ease and familiarity that flowed over whatever gashes and jaggednesses past events had revealed, she said, 'Why don't we go home now?' so they gathered themselves up and walked out into the cooler afternoon and hailed a cab. She leant gently against him in the cab, so gently and lightly that he wondered if he were not imagining it. So gently that he did not put his arm around her for fear of disturbing the delicateness, the naturalness. She had, though, to sit up and direct the driver as they got into the network of side streets near where she lived.

'Look,' she said, suddenly, pointing. 'There's Fowler.' And when they passed him she explained to the driver she'd meant him to stop. They waited for Fowler to catch them up.

'Do you want to offer him a lift?' Graham asked.

'No, it's not worth it, I can get out and walk up that short cut.'

She opened the door. 'Do you want to come in for a drink or anything,' she asked, 'or do you want to keep the cab?'

Fowler approached, his shirt open, wearing dark glasses, and carrying *Sight and Sound*.

'I might as well keep the cab,' he said.

'All right,' she said, sweetly. 'Well, come in some other time and have a drink. Thanks for the lift.' She got out and shut the door. The driver had just let in the clutch and they were moving away, when she opened the door again. They stopped. 'Oh,' she said, 'Thanks for a lovely afternoon. I do hope you don't get the sack. Don't forget my party next Friday.'

'You'd not even mentioned it, so how could I?'

'Well, I have now,' she said. 'Bring a bird if you want,' she offered, generously. And ran off smiling and waving towards Fowler.

He decided to go to Jacquie's party because it was a party. But he had no more thoughts of establishing any relationship with her, special or otherwise. She could, of course, be seen to present a challenge, but he was not interested in challenges. He half suspected that that would have been the way, that she hoped for challengers who would participate in a long strategy, whose every manoeuvre would be for her its own satisfaction; secure in the knowledge that having Fowler she had nothing especially to want, and if she misplayed the exercise and the strategist withdrew in disgust or boredom she had nothing to lose, having Fowler. He suspected, indeed, that she was deeply unimaginative, that having Fowler she contemplated no other diversion; unless it were some visiting celebrity, which would not be a diversion but a ladder shooting her up to higher snakes. Advancement to a firmer security might attract her, but a sexual detour offered no appeal. He didn't know; he might have been calumniating her. But that was how he intended to leave it.

'I don't know,' he said to Nina in the pub, having asked her to go with him, 'where this frigging party is. I've never actually been to Fowler's place. The only times I've got near it I've been stopped by disaster.'

'I thought you were on with Jacquie.'

'Like hell I was.'

'Ah,' she said. 'I'd wondered why you alone had been privileged.'

And the fact that he was just one of the many who had failed provided some consolation.

He knew as they went round trying to discover who knew where Fowler lived that he shouldn't have been doing that; he knew that the party wasn't open and that the word had deliberately not been spread around; and that they were now all too successfully spreading it around. But it seemed the easiest way to make the discovery, and he wasn't very concerned about the consequences. Though the consequences were soon upon him. Dexter called out from the fence where he was peeing when they arrived at Fowler's, 'Hey, Jacquie's looking for you. She's been waiting for you to arrive.'

He felt a sudden warmth towards her again. 'Marvellous,' he said.

'Sure,' said Nina.

And as they went on towards the door, Jacquie passed it and catching sight of them, stopped there.

'Graham Coburn, I've been waiting for you – '

He felt he should have rushed up and embraced her, but he lacked such spontaneity. Instead he limply repeated, 'Marvellous'.

But silhouetted before the lighted doorway she offered no warmth.

'Did you bring all these dreadful people, Graham Coburn? Was it you brought them all along? You've ruined my party.'

'Me?' he said. 'I haven't brought anybody, just Nina.' And was about to explain she had said he could bring a bird, but she did not wait.

'All these dreadful people,' she said, 'all the pub, you've brought all the pub and they're ruining everything.'

Inside there was just the noise of the party, sad music, no riot, no smashing furniture, no breaking glass.

'It sounds all right,' he said.

'I could kill you.'

He stood there before her. 'It sounds all right,' he said again. And then, 'I'm sorry, but I didn't bring anyone, it's nothing to do with me.'

'Of course it's to do with you,' she said.

She gave no reasons for her accusation, but was too distraught to argue with.

'What do you want me to do?' he asked, conciliatory. 'Do you want me to go?'

'What's the point of going and leaving all these hideous people behind? I don't care what you do. I could just kill you.'

And she went at that, back into the lighted rooms through which she rushed in her anger, seeing the wreckage of her party.

'We might as well go in now we're here,' Nina said.

'Honestly,' he said, 'I didn't bring anybody.'

'You don't have to defend yourself to me, dear,' she said.

Inside he couldn't see what the fuss was about, all the faces were familiar enough, there seemed no obvious outsiders. Till he realized that it was just those familiar faces from every party after the pub that were unwelcome. He tried to speak to Jacquie as she swept past, but she turned her head nobly away and ignored him. He found a bottle opener and sat on the floor, disconsolate at the accusations, at yet another loss of Jacquie. He sat a long time.

Dexter came up to him, remarked on his cheerlessness. 'What are you doing here, anyway?' Graham asked, surprised.

'Oh, I just heard it was on, you know, you hear these things. So I used your name and got in.'

'You what?'

'Well I figured you'd be here after all that *grande passion* stuff with Jacquie, so I figured that would get me in.'

'Jesus,' he said. 'What did they do?'

'They didn't do anything. What's the matter, anyway?'

'I'm up shit creek for having invited the whole pub here.'

'Did you?'

'Of course I didn't.'

'No, of course you wouldn't. But they're all here aren't they?'

'Why did you have to go and use my name?' Graham asked.

'Why not? It's a good name. It's publicity for you.'

'But Christ, why blame it on me? What am I going to do when Fowler wants to thump me?'

'Aw don't take any notice of Fowler, he's too piss weak to thump anyone.'

And it was at that moment that Fowler at last found Graham amongst the figures drinking in chairs and on the floor.

'I want to speak to you,' he said.

'Go ahead.'

'I'd rather speak next door.'

Graham raised himself from the floor. 'Don't lose the bottle,' he asked Dexter, a last gesture of ease.

They went into a totally empty room, white walls and ceiling, bare wooden floor. It had perhaps been emptied for dancing, but no one danced there.

'So I'm too piss weak to thump anyone,' said Fowler, his shadow against the white wall like the outline of his favourite screen heavy.

'I didn't say that.'

'I know you didn't, but your friend did.'

'I don't see why I should be blamed for my friends.'

'Not when you told him to come along tonight?'

'I didn't actually.'

'Nor the other two hundred bastards who came?'

'There's not even two hundred here,' Graham said, randomly.

'The numbers are irrelevant,' said Fowler. 'Whether it's fifty or five thousand, you invited them.'

'Me? I don't know five thousand people.'

'I told you, the numbers are irrelevant.'

The electric light globe hung from its flex, bare, unshaded. Nobody looked into the room though the door was ajar.

'I didn't invite anyone.'

'You just opened your big mouth to everyone in the pub.'

'Me? Why pick on me? How do you know everyone else didn't say there was a party on at the pub?'

'Because yours is the only name people used.'

'Oh for Chrissake; if they used my name it's because they're covering up for whoever told them.'

'I doubt it,' said Fowler, with a heavy certainty that swept the point away.

'But people knew there was a party on without my telling them.'

'They didn't know where it was till you told them.'

'How could I tell them? I didn't know where it was myself, I had to ask.'

'And that's not telling people?'

Graham shrugged, hopelessly.

'What's it matter anyway? They're not doing any damage. For Chrissake you've crashed enough parties.'

'I've never crashed a party,' said Fowler.

'Like hell.'

'Go on then, name a party I've ever crashed.'

'God, I don't know the details of your felonies.'

'Crashing a party isn't a felony.'

'Then what are you so worked up about?'

'Because it's trespass. Anyway, name a party I've ever crashed.'

He was about to name the Paddington one where he'd first met Jacquie, but remembered in time that it might provoke Fowler to fresh anger if he remembered Jacquie's reluctance to leave.

'Look, it's all irrelevant,' Graham said. 'I didn't invite these people.'

'Well they're here, aren't they?'

'If you say so, I suppose they are. Why don't you throw them out?'

'Because I don't like using physical violence.'

Graham remembered Dexter's comment. He hoped Fowler wouldn't, but he could tell from his·expression that he had.

'But,' said Fowler, 'I've got a bloody good mind to take a swipe at you this minute.'

'Do you want me to leave?' he said, in preference to the swipe.

'What good will that do?'

'Well what do you want me to do?'

'Just watch it, Coburn, that's all. Just watch it.'

Except for Graham, Jacquie and Fowler, and perhaps a few of Jacquie's actress friends who might have left in disgust or irritation, the arrival of the pub seemed to have affected nobody. The party was pleasantly alive. And after a few more drinks Graham even began to enjoy himself and danced with Nina till they got mildly bored with each other and looked for fresh diversions. So he moved to Kate, whose soft glowing warmth he found very sexy, which made him wonder if he'd made a mistake in opting for Nina from their joint household. If he'd had his car he would have been tempted to go off with Kate then, which might have saved a lot of trouble; but since they were both dependent on Nina for transport he rejected the idea, regretfully.

It was Kate who pointed out to him that there was going to be trouble. He looked round, noticed but for the first time registered that Nina was dancing and had been for some time with Fowler. He smiled at them, hoping it would to some degree ingratiate him with Fowler, for having brought her.

'Wrong way,' said Kate.

He turned to the other side of the room where Jacquie was sitting, curled up in a chair, watching Fowler, watching with that familiar intensity.

'Oh dear,' he said, weakly.

'Does she know it was you who brought Nina?' Kate asked.

He nodded.

While Kate was looking round for somebody with a cigarette, he went over to Jacquie. She didn't move to acknowledge his presence, but sat in her iciness, a snow child frozen into a pillar of ice, the pure white of her still amidst the ruin of her party.

'Do you want to dance?' he asked her.

'No, thank you.'

'Do you want a drink?'

'No.'

He spread his hands hopelessly over the glacial wall, but though he could see her through its transparency, he could not reach her.

'Are you tired? Do you want a cigarette?' Though he didn't have one.

'No. I don't want anything. Least of all you, Graham Coburn. You're done enough damage for one evening. Why don't you just go and get lost. Go and talk to the grotty editor of your pervy magazine.'

'Sorry,' he said.

'Don't apologize to me,' she said. 'Just don't come anywhere near me, that's all.'

He went back to Kate, his hands feeling the contours of her buttocks, her breasts; he wondered if Fowler were going to get off with Nina. In which case he might as well leave with Kate now while there was still a chance of finding a cab somewhere. But he was too tired, altogether too content to initiate anything. Eventually they went into the other room and sat down. He was surprised to find it empty. Everyone except the few couples dancing and the stray drunk who might be found in odd corners, must have left. At the end of the record Jacquie moved from her chair and advanced on Fowler. She had scarcely spoken to him all evening after his letting the gate-crashers in. She asked if he had finished dancing.

'Oh, I don't know,' he said, easily. 'Why, do you want to dance?'

'You wouldn't know since you've not asked me all evening; and it's a bit late to try and find out now.'

'Come off it, Jacquie love,' he said, 'you don't have to wait to be asked for Chrissake.'

'Don't "love" me,' she said. 'And if I did have to wait to be asked I'd wait a long time before you ever noticed.'

'Look, love, sorry, but look, I didn't know you – for Chrissake you could have danced with lots of people – Christ, even fucking Coburn wanted to.'

'Oh marvellous,' she said, 'tremendous, I'd just love to dance with even fucking Coburn.'

'You've changed your mind then from the last few times,' he tried to interject. But she cut across.

'Just so as you can try and fuck his lousy girl.'

'It's not his girl.'

'I don't care whose girl it is,' she screamed, 'but he brought her and you've spent all evening with her.'

Nina slid away into the other room, provoking in her turn Kate to drift away on some excuse and put on another record,

145

softly, out of respect for the quarrel but loud enough for a discreet muffling of it.

'Spending all evening with a girl – which I didn't anyway – doesn't mean you're trying to fuck her.'

'Well, what else were you trying to do?' And she went away.

'Hey, Jacquie, stop,' he called.

'Can't I even get my cigarettes?'

Music softly filled the room. Kate went up to Fowler and they started to dance.

When Jacquie came back some time later in that timeless early morning it was in time to hear Kate saying to Fowler, with all her generous easy warmth, as they danced scarcely moving but with much languorous stroking of hands over bodies, drawing of arms around each other, 'Why don't we go and have a fuck somewhere?'

'I can't now,' Fowler began, but whatever he was going to say was lost by Jacquie's screaming out, 'No one's stopping you, you can go and have a fuck right this minute where you are for all I care.'

Fowler stopped dancing, turned to her, began, 'Look – '

'I have been looking, don't you touch me, you oaf, I've been looking all evening, I've had nothing else to do but look.'

'For Chrissake Jacquie love – '

'Don't "love" me,' she said again.

To which he now replied, 'What makes you think I do?'

'Not much at all,' she said.

'Sorry, I didn't mean it.'

'Didn't you? People never say what they don't mean. You've spent all evening trying to get on to different women.'

'That's not true.'

'I've watched you.'

'Pity you've nothing better to do than sit around watching,' he said.

'Because it cramps your style, I suppose.'

'Look, baby,' he said, 'if I want to get on to anyone I don't spend all bloody evening at it, and my "style" isn't that bloody susceptible to cramping.'

'Oh,' she said.

'Yes.'

'Big deal. Fowler, the big screen lover.'

'Go on,' he said.

'No, you go on. Go on, tell me more; you're obviously dying to announce all your conquests. Why don't you get out your list of all the women you've got off with and read it out.'

'Sure you want it?'

She had gone an ashen white, a drained white with her fury.

'I wouldn't say I did if I didn't.'

'A complete list, or just the last twelve months?'

'The last twelve months might be more interesting,' she said. And the quaver in her voice showed for the first time her fear. For she hadn't expected it, hadn't expected the list of the women he'd slept with while all the time she'd believed he was faithful to her, and had all the time been faithful to him, she had not, right till the moment he began, expected there to be any substance to his proclaimed roll call. But as soon as he began, she accepted the awful authenticity of it, and never for one moment doubted but that it was true, never allowed the hopeless possibility that he might have been lying and have invented the list; she knew, as soon as he began, that the lying had all been done earlier, all been done in the twelve months whose fabric was now utterly destroyed, against the hurtful falsity of whose dishonest memory she threw herself, hurled the glasses and ashtrays and bottles that were on the floor beside her. 'Oh you bastard, oh I hate you, oh I could kill you,' she screamed, her frenzy distracting her so that each aim was wide, each shot enfeebled, and Fowler was able easily to dodge all the missiles, and Kate, Nina, and Graham to slip out unscathed to the car. There was no point in remaining longer; they felt embarrassed at having intruded so far. The record player stopped as they walked out of the gate, struck perhaps by something Jacquie had thrown. The only remaining sound was her sobbing. Which did not carry far in the night, it was so low. And they walked on into silence, and in the car the silence gave way to Kate and Nina singing, softly, in unison, as Graham sat between them.